AN APPLE A SLAY

A Small Town Cozy Mystery

LOUISE STEVENS

D1520815

Edited by: Trish Long's Blossoming Pages Author Services

Cover design: Elizabeth Mackey

Proofreading: Shasta Schafer

❈ Created with Vellum

Once again to my Leo.

And also to Claire Marti, without whom this book might never have been finished.

Thank you both for your unfailing support.

Chapter One

"Why don't you take that apple and stick it—" Dylan snapped at a round man whose face was as red as the piece of fruit he waved menacingly at my boyfriend.

"In some delicious melted caramel to make a tasty treat?" I jerked my head toward the group of children touring Maple Hills Orchard on a field trip.

The kids gaped at Dylan with their jaws dropped. I was right there with them because I'd been dating Dylan for three months now and I'd never seen him say a harsh word to anyone.

Dylan's eyes opened wide as he realized he had an audience. A youthful audience. "Does anyone want a free piece of maple sugar candy?" He called out in a too bright voice.

The kids all cheered and raised their hands.

"Head on over to the counter and tell the lady Mr. Carlow sent you for a free piece of candy."

The children stormed the counter, and a pang of sympathy hit me for the girl working there. I should go help her, but I wanted to stay to make sure Dylan didn't deck this guy.

"Oh, great. Candy. Just what the kids need ... more sugar." One teacher rolled her eyes at the other.

"But it's maple sugar," I said in a hopeful tone. "That's better, right?"

They turned their heads and looked at me like I was naïve, or a simpleton, possibly both. One of the women sighed and said, "Sugar is sugar. It gets them all hopped up just the same."

The seriously underpaid public school teachers dragged their heels as they followed their students to the counter.

I rushed to Dylan's side to play peacemaker if necessary, but the man turned on his heel. Balancing his bag of fruit, six-pack of hard cider, and box of maple leaf-shaped candy, he stomped toward the exit.

When I'd agreed to work part-time at Dylan's family business, Maple Hills Orchard, during their autumn busy season, I'd never expected this kind of drama. Most people came to our tiny hometown of Maple Hills, Connecticut, to peep at the colorful fall foliage and pick apples. Not to pick a fight with Dylan, aka the nicest guy in town.

"Who was that guy?" I brushed my hand over his shoulder, and it was as hard as a brick wall. Dylan's sunny nature was one of the things which attracted me to him. Okay, his good looks and swimmer's build might've played a small part too, but mostly I loved the optimistic way he approached life. I couldn't imagine what the man had done to stress him out this way.

"Dennis Millikan." Disdain dripped from his voice.

"Is he new in town since I moved away?"

I'm Amanda Seldon, and my career had taken me away from my hometown for fifteen years, until I'd returned last summer when I'd left my corporate job behind in Los Angeles and moved back East to follow my dream of being an author.

"He's a newcomer. He moved here from Chicago last year. He opened Oh Denny Boy's, a microbrewery on the edge of town."

"Oh, I've passed it. What's your deal with him?"

Dylan scowled. "He's a total jerk. He's been trying to sabotage my hard cider business." As a way to introduce a more year-round revenue stream, he had recently expanded his business to include making and selling hard cider.

"What's he doing?" I reached out and stroked his arm.

He placed his warm hand over mine, and some of the tension released from his shoulders. "Trying to pressure Hitch at the tavern and the local stores not to carry my ciders."

I glanced at the mob swarming the counter and caught my coworker's imploring gaze at me. "I've got to help her. I want to hear all about it, but can we talk about it after the field trip leaves?

Dylan waved his hands toward the candy counter. "Go. I need to get back to work too. We can go to Hitchcock's Tavern for happy hour and talk."

"Sounds good." We exchanged a quick kiss, which prompted the kids to hoot at us. My face heated as I rushed behind the counter to hand out candy to the wild-eyed children. The teachers were right. The last thing they needed was more sugar.

❧

WHEN MY SHIFT ENDED, I PACKED UP MY LAPTOP AND headed to Maple Hills Public Library to get some writing done. My lifelong friend Jeremy Patterson was editing my manuscript's first draft. Lucky for me he is a high school English teacher. While he edits it, I've moved on to researching the second book in my historical mystery series.

As I entered the library, a woman's voice bellowed from the stacks, "If it isn't my favorite niece."

"I'm your only niece, and won't hollering in the library get you kicked out of the American Library Association?"

A gorgeous brunette emerged from the stacks pushing a half-empty book cart. She threw back her head and laughed. "Only if you snitch. But seriously, Mandy-bel, it's time you abandon your librarian stereotypes and move with the times. We're not just shushers anymore."

My Aunt Lori was younger than my dad by a good bit. She was in her mid-fifties, but easily looked fifteen years younger, and nobody enjoyed life more than she did.

"I'm here to do research on book two." I plopped the tote bag on an empty table and pulled out my laptop.

"Since your parents have returned from their summer RV tour of national parks, I notice you're working here a lot more often. Are things getting crowded at their house?"

I bobbed my head from side to side. "Maybe a little. I'm used to living by myself, and Mom has drifted right back into mothering mode. I love her, but... "

"But you're in your mid-thirties. I get it. And your secret is safe with me," Aunt Lori flopped into the seat across the table from me.

"Thanks. I feel guilty even thinking it, because I adore Mom and Dad." I nibbled the corner of my bottom lip.

"Of course you do. But it doesn't mean you want to be treated like you're fifteen again. How is the search for your own place going?"

"I have an appointment tomorrow with the real estate

agent you told me about, and we're going to look at one of those new townhomes by the lake."

"Those are great. One of my friends lives there, and they're really nice. Brand new and everything is top quality."

Divorced for a couple of years, Aunt Lori's social life would put a Real Housewife's to shame, so the word 'friend' could mean anything from her wide circle of friends to one of the many men whom she casually dated. Casual, because post-divorce Aunt Lori didn't do serious. She was all about the fun.

"I'm looking forward to seeing the unit for sale. A condo would be perfect, because then I won't have to maintain the landscaping, or heaven forbid, shovel." I shuddered.

Aunt Lori snickered. "It's going to be a hoot watching you deal with your first Northwestern Connecticut winter after ten years in Southern California."

"I'm wondering how Fluffy is going to deal with it. The snow is going to be deeper than she is tall."

Fluffy was my foster fail shih tzu. She was the runt of her litter and abandoned at a shelter where I volunteered back in Los Angeles. I bottle-fed her when she was a tiny puppy and completely lost my heart to her.

"The Beast will glare and growl and even the snow will melt before her wrath," Aunt Lori intoned as if she were narrating an old-time horror film.

Did I mention Fluffy had some issues? Most everyone but Dylan and I called her The Beast. Capital T. Capital B. And her personality sometimes warranted it. But she and I were a team and, with me at least, Fluffy was a love bug.

"Hardy-har-har." I rolled my eyes, although conceding to myself my aunt might have a teeny, tiny point. After all, Fluffy's fury had helped me fight off a killer last summer.

Seriously. A murderer, but they were still no match for my Fluff.

Aunt Lori straightened her pencil skirt as she stood. "Want to hit happy hour at Hitchcock's when I get off work?"

"I'm actually meeting Dylan there later." Which reminded me about the weird altercation at the orchard earlier. "Hey, what do you know about a guy named Dennis Millikan?"

Aunt Lori had begun to push the book cart back toward the stacks but stopped and grimaced. "Ugh. I can't stand him. He's always coming on to me, and the man cannot take 'no' for an answer. Why do you ask? Is he bothering you? You're a little young for the old letch."

"No, not me. But Dylan fought with him today at the orchard."

Her perfectly shaped eyebrows shot skyward. "Dylan. Dylan Carlow? The nicest guy in Maple Hills? The one who stops his truck to let squirrels cross the street? He was fighting with someone?"

"Not fist fighting, but arguing. And in front of a school field trip full of little kids."

She snorted. "Well if anyone could drive a saint to violence it would be that jerk. Trust me, avoid him like the plague. It's a wonder no one has killed him."

"Don't even joke about it." After finding a body last summer and having been a suspect, I was not ready to joke about murder.

～

"ARE YOU SURE YOU DON'T WANT DINNER?" MY MOM stirred a pot of chili on the stove, and the tantalizing aroma of tomato, spicy peppers, and cumin wafted over to me.

Fluffy barked at the magic word 'dinner' and pranced over to my mother's feet. Mom recoiled ever so slightly.

"Honestly, Mom, she's just begging for food. She's not going to attack you."

My mother wrinkled her nose and peered down at my dog. If I were going to be completely honest, with myself if with no one else, Fluffy did have some issues as a holdover from her early days. I was pretty much the only person safe from her occasional anxiety-driven wrath.

"If you say so." She took a step away from Fluffy and spoke to her in a slow, quiet voice. The way a hostage negotiator would talk to a gun-wielding bank robber with a vault full of innocent people. "Chili is not for doggies, but I'm sure Amanda will feed you before she leaves."

I seriously needed to get my own place soon. I strolled to the fridge and pulled Fluffy's food out, which diverted her attention. With a yip of pure happiness, her claws clicked on the kitchen floor as she trotted over to me, her plumed tail waving over her back. "You're a good girl aren't you, Fluff?" I bent down and patted her head.

"To you," my mother muttered.

Picking up Fluffy's dog dish from the floor near her crate, I narrowed my eyes at my mother. "If you didn't always act like she was a bomb about to explode, she'd relax more around you too."

Mom took a deep breath. "You're right. I'm sorry. I know how much you love Fluffy, and I should make more of an effort. I just never know what's going to set her off and turn her into Franken Fluffy."

Okay, even I had to admit it was a good line. I snorted and put Fluffy's food down, and she tucked into it with relish. "Good one, Mom. I appreciate you letting us stay here until we get our own place, and I know her behavior can be a little—"

"Terrifying?"

"Challenging," I corrected Mom with a slight frown.

"One person's challenging is another person's terrifying," she said with a slight shrug. "So you never answered me, are you sure you don't want dinner?"

"Nope. Thanks though. It smells delicious. I'm meeting Dylan at Hitchcock's Tavern for happy hour, and we'll grab some of their appetizers there."

The corners of my mom's mouth tilted up as she stirred the chili. "I'm so happy you and Dylan are a couple now. He's a good man."

Butterflies danced a little conga line in my stomach. Sometimes I still couldn't believe my high school crush and I were in a relationship. Back in the day, I didn't think cool kid Dylan knew nerdy little me was alive, much less returned my feelings. It took us almost twenty years, but we were together now and still in that exciting new relationship time.

Fluffy's dog tags clanged against the bowl as she licked it to get every last bit of her dinner.

Mom turned, leaned against the counter and crossed her arms as she watched Fluffy. "She is a good little eater."

I nodded. "She's very food motivated. The fear her food will be taken away is strong."

"Mm-hmm." Mom bobbed her head. "I learned that to my sorrow, when I tried to take her empty bowl away, and she snapped at me."

Yep. Fluff and I needed our own space. Pronto. I hung my head. "Sorry about that, Mommy."

"I know, sweetie pie." She patted my shoulder as she skirted around Fluffy to start setting the table for my dad and her. "Is anyone else going tonight?"

"Aunt Lori is."

"Oh ho ho! Are Hitch and her still an item? That's got to be a record for her since the divorce. They've been dating for a few months now."

"I don't think they're exclusive or anything. Hitch is kind of the male version of Aunt Lori, so they have a lot of fun together, but I don't know if it's serious."

I glanced at the time on the microwave mounted over the stove, and gasped. "I didn't realize what time it is. I'm going to be late if I don't hustle. C'mon, Fluff, let's go outside."

As I clipped her leash onto her collar, Mom asked, "Did you get her Maple Hills dog license yet?"

"It's on my schedule this week. Between my job at the orchard and writing, I've been on the hop lately. Honestly, you'd think people from other states have never seen an apple before. The orchard has been jumping."

"Good news for Dylan's business."

"True. He had a local customer today who was kind of a tool. Dennis Millikan. He owns a brew pub or something?"

Mom nodded. "Oh Denny Boy's. Your dad and I tried it when it first opened. You know how it is in a small town, a new place is always exciting. But it wasn't my cup of tea."

"How come?" I paused at the back door.

"It was kind of tacky. Like a New England theme park or something. Not at all authentic. And Millikan was lording it over everyone there. What a blowhard." She turned back to the stove and stirred the chili.

Hmm... It seemed like my mother didn't like Dennis Millikan either. What kind of person could manage to make my kindly mother and even kindlier boyfriend dislike him so intensely?

Chapter Two

Even on a weeknight, Hitchcock's Tavern was packed for happy hour. Loud rock music blasted over the speakers, and the crowd shouted to be heard over it. I stood on my tiptoes and spotted Dylan seated at the bar. He saw me at the same moment and pointed to an empty barstool next to him.

I shoved my way to his side, greeting people as I went. I may have lived away from Maple Hills for a long time, but all the locals welcomed me home with open arms, and I was surprised by how many people I knew here now.

When I reached Dylan's side, my gaze drifted from his warm hazel eyes, which never failed to draw me in, to the platter of loaded nachos on the bar next to him. He stood up and blocked my view, but I'm fairly certain I spotted a cocktail with my name on it next to the pile of cheesy, salty goodness.

He pressed a quick kiss to my lips. "I hope you don't mind I ordered for us."

"I will never protest having nachos waiting for me

when I arrive somewhere. Anywhere, really. Even the doctor's office."

"I think the whole purpose of the doctor's office is to keep you away from things like Hitchcock's mountain of nachos." He chuckled and sat back on his barstool and slid the drink my way.

"For me?" I perched on the stool he'd risked life and limb to save for me. Seating at Hitchcock's happy hour was a cutthroat business.

"Yep. A pear vodka and tonic."

"You are a saint among men." The fizzy tonic tickled my nose as I took a sip, and then I grabbed the gooiest, cheesiest tortilla chip I could find. "Speaking of your saint-liness, tell me about this Dennis dude. My mom really dislikes him too. What's his deal?"

"Dennis? Are you talking about Dennis Millikan? I despise the man." Hitch Girard stood on the other side of the bar from us with a scowl on his usually cheerful face.

Seriously, Hitch was a laidback surfer dude who happened to live in the hills of Connecticut instead of Malibu. His shaggy brown hair had a hint of gray at the temples, and his dark brown eyes always twinkled with merriment. Except now. They were narrowed, and his lips were pressed in a straight line.

"Okay, what the heck is this guy's deal? You, and you," I pointed at each man in turn, "And my mom are the nicest people in town, and this Dennis guy manages to make all of you look like thunder."

"He's always in my face, like it's my fault the locals don't go to his ridiculous microbrewery." Hitch held up his hands palms up and raised his eyebrows as he looked between Dylan and me. "I mean, you design your business as a tourist trap, then you can't be surprised when no one but tourists want to go there, am I right?"

"Are we still talking about that obnoxious man? A plague upon his house." Aunt Lori's voice sounded behind me.

I twisted in my seat to face her. "We are. I'm just curious about him, because I haven't met anyone yet who can stand him."

Hitch slid a dirty martini across the bar to my aunt without even being asked. She beamed at him. "Bless you, Hitch. This is why I keep you around."

He threw back his head and laughed. A customer called his name from the other end of the bar, and he looked over his shoulder as he walked away. "Is that the reason?"

"One of them," Aunt Lori called after him.

Dylan stood up and gestured to his barstool. "Take my seat, Lori."

She patted my shoulder, before grabbing her glass and slipping onto the tall stool. "Oh, he's a keeper, Mandy-bel."

We enjoyed our drinks and nachos, and by unspoken consent the three of us discussed anything but Dennis Millikan. Suddenly, a ruckus sounded behind us. Angry voices were raised loud enough to be heard over the music, and everyone in the bar turned to look. Including us.

"Speak of the devil, and he shall appear," Aunt Lori said.

Dennis loomed over a table and shouted at a mousy-looking woman. "You know it wasn't my fault, but you harp on it all the time. You're ruining my good name in this town!"

Hitch rushed out from behind the bar. "You managed to ruin your name all by yourself, Millikan. Leave Bitsy alone."

"He is a charmer, haranguing a woman who looks like

she wouldn't say boo to a ghost. I'm starting to see why no one likes him." I popped another chip in my mouth and watched the scene unfolding before me.

"Shut your gob, Hitch. This has nothing to do with you." Millikan's face was as red as a ripe strawberry.

"It does when it's happening in my bar. Are you going to walk away and leave Bitsy in peace, or am I going to have to toss you out of here?" Hitch inserted himself between the woman and Millikan.

Hitch had several inches height on Dennis, and was clearly in better shape, although they were about the same age. Dennis jutted out his chin, but stepped back from the woman's table.

"I have as much a right to be here as anyone else." Millikan puffed out his chest.

Hitch's stance did not ease, but his voice was easy. "Everyone is welcome at Hitchcock's Tavern, unless they're causing trouble. Are you causing trouble, Millikan?"

"I'm just here for happy hour, like everyone else." He gestured to the packed bar with one arm.

"Things lonely at your own bar?" A man's voice called out from the crowd and was greeted with a chorus of laughter.

Millikan's face flushed again, and he clenched his fists.

"Guess that comment hit a little too close to home," Dylan whispered to me.

Not quietly enough apparently, as Millikan turned his head sharply to glare at our little group. He stomped over to us.

The woman he'd been yelling at rose, gathered her things, and scurried for the door. Hitch watched her go and shook his head, but then returned to his post behind the bar.

"Not surprised to see you here, Carlow. Kissing up to

Hitch to sell your watered-down cider here?" Millikan sneered.

Dylan took a deep breath and maintained eye contact until the other man looked away. Millikan's gaze fell on my aunt. "Lori Seldon. Of course you two are friends. And you're chasing after Hitch, aren't you? I hope you realize he's a player."

Hitch wiped down a spot on the bar with vigor, but then winked at Lori. "I'm the one doing the chasing."

The corners of her mouth tilted up, as she looked at Hitch and said, "And who says I'm not the player?"

Millikan sputtered, clearly having no idea how to respond to their banter. He'd expected to start another fight, but was doomed to disappointment.

He scowled at me. "And who are you? You're the broad from the orchard store, aren't you? New in town."

"Amanda Seldon is more of a local than you'll ever be," the man sitting next to Aunt Lori said.

I squinted at him, and then recognition dawned. "Mr. Knight? I loved your English class in high school. It's so good to see you."

"Welcome back, Amanda. Jeremy tells me you're writing a book. I'm very pleased. You always had a talent for writing."

Dennis glared back and forth between us as we spoke. "Isn't this cozy? This miserable town. If you weren't born and bred here, you're nothing but garbage, huh?"

Aunt Lori shrugged. "I imagine garbage is garbage wherever it goes."

He roared, "Are you calling me garbage?"

Wow. Happy hour had definitely taken a turn in a decidedly less happy direction.

Mr. Knight frowned. "Why don't you take it down a notch, Millikan. Dylan's brother is the police chief, and I imagine he has him on speed dial, so if you're looking for a fight, I'm sure he can get him down here in no time."

Millikan held up his hands. "I'm not looking for a fight. No need to call the cops. I've had enough of this dump anyway."

He raised his voice and looked around as he announced to the crowded bar, "I'm heading back to Oh Denny Boy's if anyone wants to join me. First drink is on the house."

His words dropped like a stone and were greeted by silence. Not even a free drink could persuade anyone to leave Hitchcock's for his bar.

"Fine. Be that way." He straightened his shoulders and strode out with as much dignity as he could muster, which granted, was not much.

"It's amazing he's lived as long as he has without being killed." Hitch shook his head.

It was the second time I'd heard that sentiment expressed today.

A WET NOSE ON MY ARM AND A LOW WHINE WOKE ME UP the next morning. Mistress Fluffy was ready to go outside. I opened one eye and peered at the time on my phone. Seven a.m. "Too early, girlfriend."

After Hurricane Dennis took his storm cloud and left Hitchcock's, happy hour had given way to karaoke, and it was late by the time I tumbled into bed. I attempted to ignore my dog, in the hopes she'd go back to sleep, but no such luck. She pawed at my arm, and her whines grew urgent.

I threw back the covers. "Fine. I'm up, I'm up."

I took a moment to run to the bathroom myself and

then just threw on a jacket over my pajamas, and slid my feet into a pair of sneakers. Fluffy stretched and trotted to the edge of the bed, where she waited for me to lift her down. With her stubby little legs, the jump off the mattress could be hazardous.

By the time we came inside, my parents were in the kitchen. Dad was fixing himself a bowl of oatmeal, and Mom held the coffee pot in her hand. "Morning, sunshine. Can I pour you a cup of coffee?"

"You are a caffeine saint among women." I gratefully took the mug after she poured it full of the aromatic, hot liquid.

"You were out with my sister last night, weren't you?" My father smirked, before putting his oatmeal bowl in the microwave.

"I was."

"Never a good idea on a weeknight," he said as he pressed some buttons on the microwave and it started it with a low hum. "Don't you have to meet the real estate agent this morning? Why would you go out with Lori the night before an early meeting?"

My head throbbed a little, and my eyes were as dry as the Sahara. I wanted nothing more than to crawl back into bed. "I didn't know Lori was coming when Dylan and I made the plans, and in my defense it was just supposed to be happy hour."

Mom took a sip of her coffee and shook her head, "It's never just happy hour with Lori. One thing leads to another, and the next thing you know—"

"You're singing a karaoke version of *Love Shack* with her and Hitch," I finished her sentence.

My parents both laughed at a volume I was not comfortable with this morning. Mom pulled her phone out of the pocket of her jeans and tapped on the screen. "I particularly enjoyed the dance routine you three did."

I gulped. "Where did you see it?"

She held up her phone and lo and behold there was a video of us singing. And dancing. Yikes.

"Nothing is secret with social media, my dear." Mom clicked out of the app and tucked the phone away.

The microwave beeped, and I winced. "I never noticed how loud that was before."

Dad pulled the bowl out and the delectable scent of cinnamon drifted through the air. I closed my eyes and breathed in deeply.

"Do you want this one? I can make myself another." He held the bowl out to me.

My stomach grumbled. "Are you sure?"

He placed the bowl on the table. "Of course. Dig in. You need to get out to see that condo this morning. Although why you're in such a hurry to move out, I don't know."

As I sipped the coffee my mother made for me, and the bowl of oatmeal my father had generously given me, I had to admit, I didn't know why I was in such a hurry either.

Mom smiled at me. "While we're both happy to have you stay here as long as you want to, I understand your need for your own space."

"We've got plenty of space," my father protested as he fixed a second bowl of oatmeal.

"She's been on her own a long time, Michael. I'm just thrilled you'll be in the same time zone with us again, let alone the same town."

"I suppose," Dad conceded grudgingly. "It is fun having you back in Maple Hills. I hope our little town doesn't seem too quiet to you after LA."

"Did you see the video, Daddy? I'm having plenty of fun here in Maple Hills."

Mom chuckled as she grabbed a yogurt out of the fridge and then sat down next to me at the table. "Maple Hills might not be small and quiet for too much longer."

"What do you mean?" I asked before shoving the last spoonful of delicious oatmeal in my mouth. Between the coffee and the stick-to-your-ribs oatmeal, I was definitely perkier than I was when I'd walked into the kitchen.

"There are rumors a development company is sniffing around town," she said in a low voice.

"Why are you whispering? There's no one but Daddy and me here."

"It's very hush-hush. Just rumors and speculation right now." She waved her yogurt spoon at me. "Perhaps you could ask your real estate agent if she has any inside scoop. What time are you meeting her?"

"Nine thirty, so I better hop in the shower." I rose and rinsed my bowl in the sink before stacking it in the dishwasher. My dog trotted after me with an accusatory gleam in her eye. "But first I need to feed Fluff. I got distracted by coffee and oatmeal. Sorry, girl."

I put fresh water in one dish and poured a tiny bit of crunchy food in her pink dish with a black dog bone painted on it. Fluffy slurped up the liquid, and then gazed up at me adoringly, with water dripping from her whiskers.

"Are you taking The Beast?" Mom peered around the kitchen island to look warily at Fluffy.

I frowned. "I wasn't going to. I'm working a shift at the orchard store after we view the condo. Why?"

"Today is the day I vacuum, and you know how wild the sound makes her."

"It does stress her out." Fluffy definitely had her issues, and the vacuum cleaner was a major nemesis in her life.

She seemed to view it as a dragon to be vanquished. "Dylan bought a crate for her at his place. I guess I could drop her there before I go to work."

"Perfect," Mom said, almost before the words were out of my mouth.

Yeah. Clearly Fluffy and I needed to get our own place.

"Okay. I'm off to try to make myself presentable." I rushed out of the kitchen with Fluffy-hot on my heels.

"Don't forget to try to get some scoop on the development from your real estate agent," Mom called after me.

"I'm on it!"

Chapter Three

I pulled my luxury hybrid sedan into a visitor space in front of a lakeside condominium. The car was a holdover from my days as a VP of human resources, because let's face it, the pay from my part-time gig at the orchard would not stretch to a ride like this one.

I really hated being late, so I'd hustled a bit and got here my customary five minutes early, but a woman in a blue blazer and black suit, with sensible pumps on her feet, stood next to a mammoth SUV. Looked like my agent was even earlier than I was.

She waved and flashed me a brilliant smile as I got out of the car, but when I lifted Fluffy out of the back seat, attached her leash, and set her down on the parking lot, the woman's smile faded.

"Amanda Seldon?"

"That's me. Hi, are you Evelyn Hochner?"

"I am. I see you brought your dog." She wrinkled her nose and looked at Fluffy like I'd brought a massive, slathering canine fresh from a dog fight ring. Okay, I admit a lot of people did view my pooch that way, but it got old.

I suppressed my sigh. "I did. If it's a problem, I can leave her in the car." Although I hated the idea, because I knew it would stress Fluffy out to no end, but I didn't really have another solution.

Evelyn screwed up her mouth. "I suppose it would be all right if you carried her."

"No problem." I scooped Fluffy up, and she pressed her velvety cheek against mine, in her doggy version of a hug.

It seemed to melt the agent's heart. "Aww, isn't she the sweetest thing." She approached us and reached out as if to pet Fluffy.

I twisted my body to form a barrier between Fluffy and Evelyn. Fluffy's lip twitched, and a low growl rumbled in her throat. Her bark and growl were surprisingly deep. "It's probably best if you don't touch her yet. It takes Fluffy a while to warm up to people."

She yanked her hand back, and her eyes were wide. "All right."

Evelyn gestured to an end-unit townhome. The Crafts-man-style condo had an attached garage and looked to be three stories. Beyond, lay the deep blue waters of the lake, sparkling like a sapphire in the bright sun on this perfect October day. "This is the unit we're looking at today. Two bedrooms, two and a half baths, and a bonus room which is really special. And as you can see, it is a lakefront property."

I was usually a practical person. Mulling over every possibility before coming to a decision on important matters, or even unimportant ones. I'll be honest, I was a world-class worrier. But this condo spoke to me. Something about it resonated with me, and the word *home* sounded in my head. "It's lovely."

"It is. Shall we go inside?" Evelyn strode to the front door, and fiddled with the lockbox to get the key.

"I can't wait to see the inside. I hope it's as gorgeous as the exterior."

"It is. All top-end fixtures." Evelyn glanced over her shoulder at me as she fitted the key in the lock. "You're living with your parents now?"

"Yes. Michael and Becky Seldon."

She tapped an expertly manicured nail on her chin. "They're the beautiful Colonial house right on Orchard Pond, aren't they? Next to the Rosenberg house?"

Apparently, her profession caused Evelyn to view her neighbors as houses rather than people. I smothered a chuckle while I pictured my parents' heads on the bodies of white Colonial houses. Sometimes my imagination got the better of me. Luckily, Evelyn had advanced into the foyer.

"That's them." I followed her inside, keeping a tight grip on Fluffy, who tensed up as we entered the condo.

"It's a fine property. If they ever want to sell, I hope they'll think of me."

"They're not planning to move anytime soon, but I'll let them know."

I gasped in pleasure as we stepped out of the foyer and into the main living area. A wall of windows overlooked the lake, and a door opened to a large deck. I hadn't even looked at the interior yet, because I couldn't drag my gaze off the scenery.

Evelyn puffed up with pride. "It's some view, right? But let me show you the rest of the unit too, because it's just as fabulous."

The kitchen was open to the living room, with white cabinets and gleaming, brand new stainless appliances. I ran my hand over the cool, smooth surface of the counter-top. "Is this granite?"

"It is. The black, white, and gray works nicely with the cabinets, I think. And as you can see, the living area has a gas fireplace, and is very roomy." She threw open a door off the foyer, which I hadn't noticed before. "A half bath on this level. The next level has virtually two master bedrooms, both with en suite baths. Although, only one looks out over the lake, so I'd make it the master if I were you. The other faces the front of the unit."

As we toured the second floor, I agreed with Evelyn. The lakeside bedroom was going to be mine. Well, mine and Fluffy's.

"One more floor, but I think you're going to be wowed by it." Evelyn waved me up the last flight of stairs.

There was only one room on this floor, the so-called bonus room Evelyn had mentioned earlier. And wowed was an understatement. I was in love. Serious, hard-core love.

The ceiling sloped on the sides, which gave it an open, lofty feel. And the wall facing the lake was all glass, framed by the ceiling into a large vee-shape.

"You're writing a book, aren't you? This room would be a perfect—"

"Writer's space," I breathed out on a sigh. I spun around, and Fluffy grunted her displeasure at the move-ment. "Sorry, girl."

"There are a couple of other units available right now, but this is the only end unit. I could arrange for us to see the others if you'd like."

I shook my head. "No need. I love this one. What do we need to do next to make it happen?"

"A decisive woman. Excellent. We can go back to my office and write up an offer?"

Since I held Fluffy, I couldn't pull out my phone. "Do you know what time it is? I need to be at work by noon."

"It's only ten fifteen. Why don't you follow me back and we can talk numbers, if you're sure. There are single family homes I can show you, and if you're not in a rush, there might be more inventory on the market in the near future." She held her finger over her ruby lips. "But you didn't hear it from me."

My mother's words from this morning popped into my head. Lost in my adoration of this condo, I'd totally forgotten I was supposed to ask her about the rumors. "I've heard some talk about a new development in Maple Hills. Is that what you mean?"

"It is. Nothing is definite yet, but from what I've heard, it would easily double or triple the population of our little town."

Since our population was roughly three thousand, her estimate was less dramatic than it would be in a bigger town, but still. "Oh my. It would change the whole nature of Maple Hills."

Evelyn heaved a deep sigh. "It would. I'm torn about it, to tell you the truth. As a real estate agent, it would open up a lot of valuable inventory, but as a long-time resident of the area, I'm afraid the town would lose a lot of its charm. Our current businesses wouldn't be enough to support that kind of population boom. I've heard talk of... " She paused dramatically before continuing in a horrified whisper, "...big box stores."

My heart sank. I wasn't good with change, and I liked our little town just as it was. "Who is behind the development? A local?"

"Heavens no. I'm not sure exactly who it is, like I said everything is very secretive, but I understand it's a New

York development firm, looking to invest big here in Maple Hills."

"Big investment in our community is good, but I hope it doesn't destroy everything positive about Maple Hills in the process."

I opened the door to the outbuilding that housed the Maple Hills Orchard offices. Knowing Fluffy's second favorite person in the world after me—fine, the *only* other person in the world she liked—was inside, she trotted ahead of me like a little big shot.

"Dylan! I have the best news—"

I stopped in my tracks when I saw he was in a meeting with someone. And not just any someone, a willowy blonde who resembled a Scandinavian supermodel dressed like a businesswoman for a photo shoot.

"Amanda, come in." Gratitude flashed in Dylan's hazel eyes. It was just for a second, and then he got his polite face back in place.

"I'm sorry, I didn't mean to interrupt."

"No problem, we were just wrapping up," Dylan said.

"Dylan is being polite; we still have some business to conduct." A brief pause before the word 'business' and the teasing tilt of her red lips was just enough to hint it was monkey business they were conducting. But I knew Dylan well enough to know this woman was no threat to me.

"Amanda, do you remember Mallory Davisson from high school? Mallory, this is Amanda Seldon."

Memories of interactions with Mallory flooded my mind, and let me just say none of them were pleasant. She'd been the quintessential mean girl when we were kids, and she seemed to save a lot of her premium nastiness for my friends and me. At the time, I didn't understand, but with an adult appreciation of the situation, I realized she was probably insecure and felt the need to go after the weakest members of the pack. Jeremy, Cara, and me.

Maybe I matured with age, but the sweeping look of condescension she gave my outfit was vintage Mallory. "Don't you look, um, sweet."

My clothes were perfect for working all afternoon in old apple barn with no central heating. I wore jeans with a pink, fuzzy alpaca sweater, and shearling boots. Not the height of fashion, but it was functional and I knew I looked cute. Although when I looked at her black pencil skirt and fitted white silk blouse, not to mention the mile-high pumps with their tell-tale red sole, a little flutter of unease in my belly made me wish I was dressed in some of my LA clothes.

I squared my shoulders and decided to be the better person. "And you look fantastic, Mallory."

She leaned back in her chair, and I could see the white all around her ice-blue eyes. Huh. Seemed like the mean girl didn't know how to react to kindness in response to her backhanded compliments. Good to know.

Her eyes narrowed. "I see you never managed to leave Maple Hills. I live in Manhattan now."

Dylan took a breath to intervene, but I sent a glance his way to let him know I had this, and his shoulders relaxed.

"I lived in Brooklyn, when I worked in Manhattan. So much more cutting-edge, you know? But I've spent the last ten years in Los Angeles. I just recently moved back to Maple Hills."

A sudden cough told me Dylan had just smothered a chuckle, and I flashed a smile his way. "And I'm very happy to be here."

"Of course you are, bless your heart."

Oh no she didn't. Did Mallory just bless-your-heart me? It was on.

She continued before I could speak. "I believe your two friends still live here too. What did everyone call you? The Three Stooges?"

I didn't enjoy conflict, and my heart thudded in my chest, but I pasted on a smile. "Oh no, it's the Three Musketeers, but I understand the literary allusion is above some people's heads."

Mallory sat up straight, and the movement diverted Fluffy's attention from her beloved Dylan, at whose feet she sat. My fierce little defender sensed a threat and growled in a manner worthy of a rottweiler and then charged at Mallory, barking wildly. Her tail was down, a sure sign she was seriously displeased.

Mallory curled up in her seat, as best she could in her tight skirt. "Call off your mutt."

"Fluffy, it's okay, sweetie. She can't hurt me," I crooned to Fluffy, but still held on tight to her leash. Sometimes there was no soothing her when she got in a state.

Dylan squatted, held out his hand, palm side up, and spoke in a calm, quiet voice, "Come here, Fluffy."

It was enough to divert her, and the barking stopped as she glanced over her shoulder to Dylan. Her tail was still down though, so it could go either way.

"Good girl. Come here." He rubbed his thumb and forefinger together and smiled at Fluffy.

Her tail slowly lifted over her back, and with one last look of disdain at Mallory, she turned and pranced to Dylan, who scooped her up in his arms. His glance at Mallory was cold. "Fluffy is not a mutt. Not that there's anything wrong with mutts."

Since I still held her leash, when Dylan picked her up, I had to move closer to his side.

"It's almost time for my shift at the orchard store, and while I'd love to stay and catch up with Mallory..." I paused briefly here, waiting for lightning to strike me. "I was wondering if I could get the key to your house, so I can leave Fluffy there while I work."

"Sure, but why can't she stay at home?" He handed the dog to me, and dug in his pockets for his key chain.

"Mom is vacuuming, and it whips Fluffy into a frenzy."

A slow smile oozed across Mallory's face like an oil slick. "You live at home with your parents? How precious."

I ignored her and turned my gaze to Dylan. "Which brings me to my good news. I just made an offer on a lake-side condo. Fingers crossed!"

His smile warmed me down to my toes. If only he could smile at me that way the whole time I was working in the chilly barn, I wouldn't need to wear these boots.

"Great news. You can tell me all about it at dinner tonight." Dylan leaned down and pressed a kiss to my lips.

Mallory cleared her throat in a pointed manner, and he reluctantly pulled away from me. "I just need to see Mallory off, and then I'll check on Fluffy before I come over to the apple barn to see you."

"See me off? We're not done with our meeting." Mallory frowned.

"Oh, yes we are," Dylan said in a firm tone, which left no room for discussion.

I snatched the key and dashed for the door, still holding Fluffy in my arms. She took the opportunity to growl one more time at Mallory, who flinched.

The woman had tormented me from the time we started school until high school graduation, and I wish I could be a better person, but the way our reunion had gone today, my only thought was karma was sweet.

Chapter Four

My spoon clanked in the bowl as I savored my last mouthful of hearty beef stew. Dylan's house was filled with the savory scent, but also cinnamon and apples.

I sniffed the air. "I understand why the house smells like this delectable stew, but what's with the cinnamon and apple scent?"

He chuckled as he stood up and reached forward to take my bowl. As he carried our dishes to the sink, he jerked his head toward the counter. "Two slow cookers, no waiting. The stew is in one and mulled apple cider is in the other. I thought we could have it after dinner, by the fire."

The picture he painted, of us snuggled in front of the cozy fire on a cool October night was lovely, but the notion of drinking apple cider after spending my days surrounded by the sights, sounds, and tastes of apples was less appealing. My dad always said I was not a poker face, and he must be right.

"Or not," Dylan said. "Are you getting sick of apples?"

My emotional radar pinged at his intense expression.

He wasn't just talking about fruit here. Was he wondering if I was sick of dating an apple farmer?

"Of course not. I love apples, and the orchard, it's just..."

His shoulders lowered, and he nodded. "I get it, it's a lot of apples. Apple muffins for breakfast, chicken salad with apples for lunch, applesauce with dinner, and apple pie for dessert. It's how I grew up, but I can see where it could be too much."

I stood and strolled over to him at the sink and bumped him away with my hips. "You cooked; I'll clean. It's the deal, remember? Why don't you tend to the fire and pour our ciders. This shouldn't take long."

"Leave the leftovers in the cooker. I'll just put it in the fridge and turn it back on warm tomorrow morning. It will be a good lunch for me."

Fluffy had already eaten, thanks to Dylan's thoughtfulness. When he'd bought the crate to keep at his house, he also picked up food bowls, her favorite flavor of dog food, and a bed, in which she was currently snoring by the fireplace.

Once the dishes were done, and we were snuggled on the sofa with our mulled cider, which actually was delicious, I had to ask. "Not to introduce a whole bunch of negativity to our otherwise perfect evening, but what business do you have with Mallory?" He hesitated, and I rushed to add, "Of course, if it's none of my business just tell me, and we'll drop the subject."

"It's not that I don't want to tell you, but Mallory stressed it was top secret. I would love to talk to you about it though."

I mimed zipping my lips. "I can keep a secret. It was kind of a job requirement when I was in human resources."

"I know you can. Okay, here goes. Mallory works for Nesbitt Sharpley-Smythe. According to her, she's virtually his right-hand person."

I tried to whistle, but it had never been a skill I could claim, and it came out more like a squeaky exhale. "He's a gazillionaire. No wonder she can afford those shoes."

"I don't know about her shoes, but I'm sure she's in a top income bracket working for him."

"So what does Nesbitt Sharpley-Smythe's right-hand person want to do with you? Professionally, I mean." Personally, I could tell she wanted to climb him like a tree, but I left that thought unspoken.

"He has his fingers in lots of pies, and one of his subsidiaries does real estate development."

"He's the developer looking at Maple Hills?" I exclaimed a little too loudly. Fluffy even lifted her head and stared at me blinkily, before realizing nothing was wrong and nestling back into her bed with a huff.

"Word's already out on the street about it?"

I rolled my eyes. "It's Maple Hills. What do you think?"

"I think the regulars at the Sit and Sip and Shear Madness probably know more about it than I do." He mentioned our local coffee shop and hair salon, both major centers of gossip.

"I haven't actually heard any details, just that a developer has been looking at the town, and the project is mega-huge. Like triple our population huge."

"Does the grapevine know where they want to build?" Dylan furrowed his brow.

"I haven't heard anything about the location. Why?"

He inhaled deeply through his nose. "Mallory came today to feel me out about selling off my land for the development."

"How many acres?"

"All of them, they want to buy the whole orchard." He clamped his jaw shut with an audible click of his teeth.

My heart pounded in my chest. "But what about your business? And your home?"

"They want all of it. I'd be unemployed and homeless."

"Hopefully, I'll be a homeowner soon, so you could crash with Fluffy and me," I said half-jokingly. The idea of living with Dylan had a certain appeal, but it was too soon in our relationship.

"The number she mentioned had so many zeroes I'd never have to work another day in my life." Dylan pursed his lips and blew out a breath.

"Which obviously doesn't appeal to you."

"I mean what would I do? I run an orchard. It's what I've wanted to do all my life, and I'm already living my dream. It would change our entire town, and I don't think it would be for the better."

"Then tell them no."

He leaned forward to put his cider mug on the coffee table, and then ran his hand over his mouth. "It's not that simple. I should've added a little rum to our cider."

I put my mug down too and rubbed his shoulders, which were as hard as cement. "You're so tense. Talk to me."

"The business is mine legally, one-hundred percent. My parents gifted it to me when they retired, with Danny's blessing. He always knew what he wanted to do, and it was most definitely not running the orchard. But I still think of it as a family business. And family land. I can't just turn down an offer that could change my whole family's lives, no matter how much I want to."

"Have you talked to them about it? Maybe they won't be interested either."

"There hasn't been time. I texted them and said I needed to discuss something about the orchard. We have a family meeting tomorrow. Danny is coming over to my house, and my parents will be on Zoom. You're off work tomorrow, right?"

My mulled cider churned in my belly, and my mind raced. There was no way I wanted to be part of his family meeting. Our relationship was most definitely not at the point where I would be sitting in on important family discussions about their finances.

"I am." My voice squeaked. I cleared my throat and continued. "But Cara wants to see the condo I made the offer on, so we're going there after she drops off the kids, and then I need to get some writing time. Plus, I don't think we're there yet. Someday, but—"

He held up his hands. "I wasn't asking you to come to the family meeting. I agree 100 percent. I just wanted to talk to you after and was wondering where you'd be."

The tightness in my chest eased, and I exhaled with a whoosh. "Cara and I are doing a drive-by at the condo and then going to the diner for breakfast. After that, I'll probably be at my parents' house."

"I'll text you when we're done, and maybe we can get together to talk."

"Of course."

"And in the meantime, I know the Three Musketeers share everything, but please don't tell Cara about Mallory's offer."

It wouldn't be easy not to gripe about Mallory Davisson's return to Maple Hills, but I knew how important it was to Dylan for me to keep mum about this deal. I crossed my heart. "I swear, I won't tell anyone a thing until you give me the all clear."

He turned to face me on the comfy, overstuffed sofa, "Now, tell me all about the condo. Do you have pictures?"

"I LOVE IT, AMANDA. THE LOCATION IS PERFECT. I JUST wish we could get inside."

Cara eyed the real estate agent's lockbox with a gleam in her eye.

"No. We are not starting the day with a little breaking and entering into my potential new home. I have a ton of pics of the inside on my phone; I'll show them to you over breakfast."

"Party pooper."

"I can see the headlines now... *Local Eye Doctor's Wife Arrested for B&E*."

"Can we at least walk around and see the back? Do you have lake access?" Cara's expression brightened.

"We can, and I do. There's a dock and a nice deck. Two decks, actually. A smaller one off the master and a big one off the living room." We walked around the side of the building as I spoke.

When we rounded the corner and Cara saw the lake view for the first time, she clasped her hands together and gasped. "It is a-freaking-mazing." She pivoted to look back at the condo. "And this deck! The parties we can have here will be epic. Are you going to get a sailboat? The kids would love it. OMG, this place is perfect."

"For you or for me?" I asked in a wry tone.

"*Tous pour un, un pour tous,*" Cara called out as if making a toast.

"So my home would be a 'one for all and all for one' kind of place for the Three Musketeers?"

"You betcha," Cara said and flashed me a cheeky grin.

The smile faded from her face as she squinted into the morning sun at a pile of debris a few condos down from mine. Um ... from the one I wanted to buy. I really needed to not let myself get too attached to this place before the papers were signed and it was officially mine.

I shaded my eyes and looked where she pointed. "It looks like someone dumped garbage there or something. Yuck."

Fluffy had been standing with her little face turned up to catch the warmth of the sun, but my pointing jerked her leash and caught her attention. She sniffed the air, and took off like a rocket toward the pile of trash. She dragged me along behind her, and Cara followed hot on our heels.

"This dewy grass is going to ruin my new boots," she groaned.

"And Fluffy's belly is so low to the ground, she's going to be soaked, and I don't have a towel in my car."

"I have one in my gym bag. We can dry The Beast off with it," Cara offered.

Now there's a true friend for you. In the *tous pour un, un pour tous* spirit, she was willing to share her own personal towel with Fluffy. Letting her kids swim off my dock in the summer was the least I could do for a friend who'd share her towel with my wet dog.

Speaking of Fluff, she was bound and determined to get to what appeared to be a bunch of clothes on the grass. "I haven't seen her this interested in something since... " My voice trailed off as we got close to the garbage, and I clutched Fluffy's leash and pulled her to an abrupt stop.

Cara skidded to a halt next to me. "What's wrong? Is that a bunch of laundry or something? Jeez, a nice complex like this, you'd think they'd have strict rules about keeping your lawn free of garbage.

"I don't think it's garbage." I shook my head slowly.

"Then what is it?"

No, no, no. Not again

I gulped. "I'm pretty sure there's a body in those clothes."

"You mean like a dead body?" Cara shrieked.

"It's definitely a person, and your screech would've woken them up if they're asleep."

"Sorry, I'm a little freaked out here. Maybe he's just passed out?" Cara inched closer.

Fluffy grunted and tugged on the leash, and I tightened my hold so she couldn't maneuver far. I really didn't want to pick her up when she was drenched with cold, wet dew. We stepped up next to Cara.

She held her hand over her mouth, and her whisky-brown eyes were wide. "Hello, sir?"

"I don't think he can hear you."

"I'm calling nine-one-one." Cara dug through her handbag for her phone.

"Good idea." I forced myself to look more closely at the man on the ground to see if he was still alive and might need CPR.

Cara started to speak to the nine-one-one operator, and then paused to look at me. "They need the address. Do you know it?"

I told her the address as I reluctantly picked Fluffy up and tucked her under my left arm like a little, furry foot-ball. I squatted next to the man and turned my body to keep Fluffy as far away from him as possible . It was a little tricky balance-wise, and I wobbled a bit.

I touched his wrist with a shudder. He was cold as ice, and damp from the dewy grass. His arm was stiff.

"They want to know if we can do CPR, while we wait for the EMTs." Cara held the phone away from her face and called out to me.

I snatched my hand back and awkwardly stood up, still clutching Fluffy under my arm. I shook my head at her. "There's no point. He's gone. And I think it's been a while. He's..."

"He's what?"

"Stiff. His body is stiff." Nausea burbled in my stomach, and I was glad I hadn't eaten breakfast yet.

Cara stared at me, frozen in place, with a wide-eyed expression of horror. Finally, she shook her head briskly and pulled herself together to answer the operator. "He's dead."

The voice sounded through the speaker. "Do you know who it is, ma'am? Can you tell what happened?"

"I don't know, maybe a heart attack?" She said to the operator and then asked me, "Can you tell who it is, Amanda? I'm trying not to look too closely."

I dragged my gaze to his face and gasped.

It was Dennis Millikan, and on the ground next to him were a half-eaten apple and an open bottle of Maple Hills Orchard hard cider.

Chapter Five

Wood grated against wood as Cara scooched her Adirondack chair on the dock, so her back was to the scene unfolding behind us. I sat in the chair opposite her, with Fluffy on my lap, wrapped in Cara's gym towel. Fluffy was tense beneath my hands as I stroked her non-breed standard curly fur, and she stared fixedly as the police and EMTs did their jobs.

"I know you're a pro at this, but I can't look at it." Cara's face was pale.

"A pro?" My voice squeaked. "I found one body last summer, I hardly think it makes me a pro."

"You have more experience than me in this sort of situation though." She swallowed hard.

I shook my head. "Trust me, this is not an area where I want to have an edge."

"Although this is different, I mean last summer when you found the body it was murder. This time he must've had a heart attack or something."

A suspicion pricked at the back of my mind, but I forced it down. Not every dead body was murder. In fact, the vast majority of the time death came from natural causes. "He seemed to have anger issues. I only met him twice, and both times he was arguing with people. It can't have been good for his blood pressure."

"But still, he wasn't that much older than us, was he?"

I scrunched up my nose. "Maybe ten or fifteen years? I'm not sure."

"It could happen to any of us, anytime. It's unsettling." Cara shuddered. "Do you mind if we skip breakfast when Danny tells us we can leave? I want to go to Mitch's office and hug him. For three or four hours."

"Your husband takes excellent care of himself. He runs several times a week and eats right. I don't think he's going to kick the bucket anytime soon."

Cara inhaled deeply, and a hint of color came back into her cheeks. "That's true, but I still want to go see him."

"I understand. I might swing by the orchard to see Dylan. We can do breakfast another time."

Our conversation had drawn my attention from the police activity, so I jumped when Fluffy sat up and growled. A glance over my shoulder told me Chief Carlow, aka Dylan's older brother Danny, approached us. His footsteps thudded on the dock.

"When will The Beast ever get used to me?" He carefully positioned himself behind my friend.

"Using Cara as a shield?" A smile played at the corner of my lips.

"My police training taught me to assess a threat, and your dog is most definitely a threat to me." His eyes twinkled, but I noticed he stayed behind Cara. "I wanted to let you know you're both free to leave."

Cara jumped to her feet. "Great! Let's go, Amanda."

She was several steps along the dock by the time she finished her sentence.

"I know it's upsetting, and I'm sorry your day started this way. But, do you mind if I talk to Amanda alone for a minute?"

"Sure." Cara stopped, and her gaze darted between the sanctuary of the parking lot and me on the dock.

Danny jerked his head toward the lot, and said in a gentle voice, "Go on ahead, Cara. We'll only be a couple of minutes."

"Okay, but this is a heart attack or something, you can't possibly suspect Amanda of murder again," she called over her shoulder as she jogged away from us.

"Yeah," Danny drew out the word. "About that ... what do you think, Amanda?"

"I'm going to go on the assumption you don't want to know what I think about being a murder suspect again. For the record, I think it would stink. You're asking what I think about the cause of death?"

He chuffed out a low laugh. "You're not a suspect this time. But, being the first person on the scene, I wanted to know what your thoughts were. You had good instincts last summer with the case at the theater, and I'm interested in what you have to say about Millikan." He sat in the seat Cara had vacated and looked out over the lake while I mulled over how to respond.

I inhaled deeply and finally answered. "I'm not as certain as Cara it was a heart attack."

He turned his head sharply to train a laser gaze on my face. "And why do you think so?"

"He obviously had been there a while, because he was, y'know..." I swallowed deeply to fight a sudden surge of nausea. Cara might think I was a pro, but finding my second body in three months was not a pleasant experience.

"Stiff?" Danny prompted gently.

"Yeah, that. And I know from taking Fluffy for her last trip outside last night, it was chilly. And he was in a tee shirt and pajama-type pants. Like he was in for the night, maybe even ready for bed. So why would he go outside to apparently eat an apple and drink an iced cider on a cold evening in those clothes? It just struck me as odd."

"Me too." Danny bobbed his head. "See? You have good instincts. I think an autopsy is in order."

"I didn't see any blood or wounds, although to be honest, I was trying to *not* look at him as much as possible. What do you think happened?"

"Maybe poison, and I don't like that idea at all."

"Why not?"

"Because he was eating an apple and drinking a cider from my family's orchard. And he's known to have a contentious relationship with my brother. I think I might have to recuse myself and hand this case over to the state police."

My heart stopped for a moment and then pounded. "So I'm off the hook, but Dylan might be a suspect this time?"

"If it's poison, it sure seems like someone wants Dylan to be suspected, and I don't like it one bit. Especially if someone else is in control of the investigation."

A horn tooted from the parking lot, and I glanced in that direction. "Sounds like Cara is getting impatient."

We both rose, and Danny jerked his head toward the parking lot. "You go on ahead. If the state police take over, they might have more questions for you. Especially given your relationship with Dylan."

I'd taken a couple of steps, still holding Fluffy, since she was a teensy bit antagonistic toward Chief Carlow. "You don't mean I really *will* be a suspect again? I was home with my parents last night after I had dinner at Dylan's."

He shook his head. "You never know what an investigator will think, especially someone who doesn't know all the players as well as I do. But I just meant the new investigator will probably want to talk to you personally, as you're the one who found him." He paused and continued in a too casual voice. "Speaking of your dinner with Dylan last night, he said he told you about the offer on the Carlow land."

"He did."

"What do you think about it?'

"I think it's none of my business. It's a Carlow family matter," I said in a firm tone of voice.

"But you must have an opinion. I mean, my brother and you are tight. Someday—"

"Is not today." I interrupted. "I'll support Dylan with whatever decision you guys come to. What do you think about it?"

"It's a lot of money. But that land has been in our family for generations. Heck, my house is built on it. Just between us, I'm not thrilled about the idea of the development in general, aside from the fact they'd want to destroy my family's legacy to build it."

"I'm not either," I admitted. "It would change Maple Hills completely."

"Very true, and I like being the police chief of a small town. I don't want to have to deal with all the problems and increased crime a bigger population brings with it."

Cara laid on the horn, and Fluffy barked as I glanced toward the parking lot. "I really better run."

"You go. Maybe we're both wrong. I'm hoping Millikan died of natural causes, and we won't have to worry about Dylan being a suspect in a murder investigation."

"Fingers crossed," I said as I quickened my pace.

But I could tell neither of us really believed it.

"Hi, is Dylan here?" I walked into the apple barn, which was where the orchard's seasonal shop was located. When Cara dropped me at home, both my parents were out, so I left Fluffy comfy and secure in her crate and headed straight here to see Dylan. His brother's fears about him being a suspect had been contagious, and I wanted to see him.

The young woman working the register looked up from her customer, her brow furrowed. "What are you doing here, Amanda? Today is your day off."

"I know. I just needed to see Dylan, and he wasn't at the office. Do you know where he is?"

"I'm not sure. Maybe he's out in the orchard?" She smiled at the lady checking out, and handed her a bag of apples. "Do you want your receipt, Mrs. Van Dyke?"

The woman looked to be twenty years older than me. Maybe around my Aunt Lori's age, but it showed more on her than it did on Lori. Her hair was a mousy gray-brown mixture, and lines were tight around her mouth. "Thank you."

When she spoke, her voice was quiet and a little squeaky, further cementing the image of her looking like a mouse forever in my mind.

She bumped into me and gasped. "Oh dear, I'm so sorry. I didn't see you." Recognition dawned in her eyes. "You're Michael and Becky's girl, aren't you? Your mother told me you'd moved back to town. She's over the moon about it."

"I am. Amanda." I held out my hand to her, and she awkwardly shifted the bag of apples and shook mine. Her hand was cold as ice, as the barn didn't have central heating and was a chilly spot.

"I'm Bitsy Van Dyke. I went to school with your Aunt Lori."

So, my instinct was correct, and she was the same age as my aunt. I smiled and leaned a little closer. "She must've been a devil back then. You'll have to tell me all about her sometime."

She giggled. "She still is a bit of a devil. I work in Maple Hills Town Hall. Next time you're there, stop by, and I'll tell you some tales."

"Amanda, I tried to reach you, and I was hoping you were on your way here." Dylan's voice sounded from the entrance to the barn.

I turned to see him bundled up for outside work, but with his arms open wide. Without hesitation or shame I ran into them and relaxed into his warm embrace.

"My brother called to tell me Dennis Millikan was dead and you found his body. I'm so sorry."

A loud gasp rent the air, and there was a thump.

Had someone fainted? I turned to see Bitsy Van Dyke still standing, but her eyes bulged and she held her hands over her mouth.

Her bag of apples was on the floor at her feet, fruit tumbled everywhere. She looked down at the ground as if she hadn't even realized she'd dropped the bag. "I'm so sorry, Dylan. Look at the mess I made," she dithered as she squatted to get the apples.

"Don't worry about these. We'll get you a fresh bag,"

Dylan said in a soothing tone, which reminded me of how he talked to Fluffy when she was anxious.

Bitsy stood up and brushed her skirt in a fluttering motion, and I noticed her hand tremble. "That's very kind of you. Thank you."

"I'm sorry, Bitsy. I didn't realize you were here. I wouldn't have blurted the news about Dennis out if I had known."

"It's all right, it was just a shock." Her voice was stronger, and she squared her shoulders and stood up tall. Well, as tall as a woman who was five feet nothing could stand.

"Of course it was," Dylan said. "Would you like to sit down?"

"No. I'm fine now." She jutted out her chin. "I can't pretend to be sad about it. I'm glad the man is dead."

The mouse had turned into a lion. I glanced at Dylan, and he didn't look as shocked to see it as I was.

The awkward moment was broken when the young woman who was working brought over a fresh bag of apples to her. "Here you go, Mrs. Van Dyke."

"Thank you, dear." Her lips pressed into a tight line, and worry shone in her eyes. "News is going to spread around town. I'd better hurry home, so Adrian doesn't hear about it from someone else."

She scurried past us and out the door.

"What on earth was that all about? And who's Adrian, her husband?" I asked.

Dylan shook his head. "Her husband left town years ago. Adrian is her son."

"Why would she have to be the one to tell him about Dennis Millikan dying?"

"Because Adrian was severely injured in a drunk driving

accident, and he hasn't been the same since. He'd been at Oh Denny Boy's Microbrewery the night it happened. Bitsy has always blamed Millikan for overserving him."

"How awful." I heard the sound of gravel flying as Bitsy's car sped out of the parking lot.

"Why don't we head over to my house for a cup of coffee, so we can talk."

"Sounds good," I murmured and followed him out the door.

He clasped my hand in his and squeezed it. "You're freezing."

"It's a cool day."

"I don't think you're just cold. I'm worried you might be having a delayed reaction to finding Millikan. My brother told me you handled it like a champ, but it had to have been upsetting."

"I'm not gonna lie. It was. But something else is bothering me right now."

"Really, what?"

We strolled around the corner of the barn and down a path through rows of apple trees toward Dylan's house.

I glanced up at him. "I noticed Bitsy didn't ask how Dennis Millikan died. He was a seemingly healthy, middle-aged man, who you wouldn't expect to drop dead. Don't you think it's funny she didn't ask what happened?"

He stopped short and turned to face me. "You're right. It is weird. Especially since Danny told me he thinks Millikan might've been murdered. Are you trying to say you think Bitsy might've killed him?"

"She certainly had cause to hate him, and she said she was glad he was dead. I mean, she doesn't seem like a killer, but you never know what someone is capable of if they're pushed too far. Even a mousey little woman like Bitsy."

WE ENTERED DYLAN'S OFFICE. "THANKS FOR TAKING THE time to talk to me. I know you have a lot on your mind right now, and I appreciate it. Would you like a cup of coffee?"

"Yes, please."

He popped a pod into the machine, pressed a button, and it hummed to life. As the fragrant coffee spurted into a white mug with the red apple logo for Maple Hills Orchard on it, he turned around. "Danny says he talked to you a little about the family situation this morning."

"He did, but we didn't talk for long. How did the family meeting go?"

Dylan fixed my coffee the way I like and handed me the mug, before setting up the machine to make his. I cupped the mug in both hands and sat in the guest chair by his desk.

"We all seem to be on the same page, which is good. But it's so much money to turn down. I'm just worried they're saying what I want to hear and not telling me what they really want."

Dylan stirred creamer into his mug and then skirted by me to sit at his desk. He flopped into the seat with a deep sigh.

"Did anyone say anything to make you think they're not being up front with you?"

"No. It's just a big responsibility, and I don't want my feelings about the land and the orchard to influence their decisions. They all know how much it means to me. And Mallory made it clear the orchard is the only land with enough acreage in Maple Hills for their development. If I turn down the offer, what if I'm holding back the town from opportunities?"

I sipped my coffee. "I can't speak for everyone, but I like the town the way it is. And I think your brother feels the same way. This development may not be popular with the locals. Even my real estate agent is torn about it. I think a lot of people won't want Maple Hills to change."

"But nothing can stay the same forever."

"No." I shook my head. "But change doesn't have to come in one dramatic fell swoop either. What Mallory's company is proposing sounds pretty radical."

"True. Maybe they could consider a smaller scale project on someone else's land. I'll talk to Mallory about it tonight at dinner."

I choked on my coffee, and it burned my sinuses.

"Are you okay?" Dylan put down his mug and moved to rise.

"I'm fine," I croaked out and flashed a thumbs-up sign. "A little coffee just went down the wrong way."

When you told me you were having dinner with a mean girl who looks like a Swedish supermodel.

He lowered himself back into his seat, and his tone of voice was dubious, "Okay."

"Anyway, so you're having dinner with Mallory?" We were too old to play games, so I decided to just ask the question I wanted answered.

He rolled his eyes and snorted. "She wanted to meet again after I talked to my family and suggested dinner tonight. Believe me, it wasn't my choice, I just want to get it over with."

"Jeremy and I are going to the diner tonight. Where are you and Mallory going?"

His hazel eyes twinkled. "Sunnyside Up Diner. Mallory was not pleased with my choice. I think she wanted something a little more elegant. But I wanted to stay local and go someplace where we could each take our own cars. I told her you and I are together, but I'm picking up some signals from her... "

"Like she's interested in you and doesn't care if you have a girlfriend?" I offered as an end to his sentence after his voice trailed off. "Color me not at all surprised."

He laughed. A deep, hearty sound that warmed me up more than the coffee. "Yeah, that's exactly what I meant. But, I'm not interested, and I knew you had plans tonight, so I figured what the heck. You don't mind do you?"

Since he was so honest with me about this meeting, and ... well, everything, I was able to reply without hesitation. "Nah. I'm just sorry you have to sit through dinner with her. From the 'Maple Hills is a tiny place' file, it's funny I'll be eating at the same restaurant."

His eyes lit up, "Maybe we'll see each other there."

"Maybe. I bet Mallory would enjoy seeing Jeremy and me." I planted my tongue firmly in my cheek, opened my eyes wide, and tried to look innocent.

"Yeah ... no." Dylan chuckled. "Is Eric having dinner with you guys?"

"No, he had to go into Manhattan today for a business meeting." Eric was Jeremy's husband and a graphic artist, who was able to work from home most of the time, but occasionally had to brave the long drive into New York City for meetings and the like. "But, I think it would still be just the two of us even if he wasn't busy. We're getting together because Jeremy said he was done editing my manuscript and wanted to discuss it."

Dylan studied my face. "You sound scared. Why? Did he say he doesn't like it?"

"He hasn't really said anything about it, which is worrying me, because you know Jeremy has never had an unexpressed thought. I expected him to just email the manuscript back to me with his comments, which I could then read and digest at my own pace. But he said he wanted to meet first."

"Okay, that does sound a little ominous, but maybe he just wanted an excuse to hang out with you on a night Eric wasn't home for dinner?"

I nibbled my bottom lip. "Or maybe he's going to tell me I'm the worst author in the history of the written word."

Chapter Six

The jukebox at the diner blasted music that would've been considered oldies when my parents were young, now I guess you could call them ancient oldies. My nerves had caused me to arrive even earlier than I normally do for my dinner with Jeremy.

I drummed my fingers on the table as I looked around. It didn't look like Dylan and Mallory were here yet. He'd gotten called away on some orchard matter, and we'd never gotten around to talking about what time his appointment was. It made me feel better to think of it as a business appointment, but I was fairly certain Mallory was thinking of it as a date. As long as Dylan wasn't, it was all good.

Sunny, the namesake owner of the Sunnyside Up Diner approached my booth. "You on your own tonight, kiddo?"

Her hair was styled the same way it had been for as long as I can remember. Bleached platinum blonde and teased in a way that added a few inches to her height.

Sunny was the heart and soul of the diner, and as cheerful as her name suggested.

"I'm meeting Jeremy for dinner, just early as always."

"It's good to be prompt." Sunny glanced at the door. "Looks like he's here now. I'll get you a diet cola and an iced tea with extra lemons for Jeremy. Be right back."

She bustled off to get our drinks, and Jeremy slid into the booth across from me. "C'mon, Amanda, give a guy a break. I got here five minutes early, determined to arrive at the same time as you, and you're already seated. Did you order too?" He rolled his eyes.

"I can see why the high school asked you to teach drama as well as English." I paused and then added, "And just our drinks. Although I didn't have to order them, Sunny just knew what we wanted."

The lady in question arrived at the table and put our glasses down. "Here ya go. I told the waitress I'd handle this order." She closed her eyes, held her fingers to her temples, and hummed. "Let me see. I'm getting a vision. Amanda will have a turkey club on whole wheat toast, and Jeremy wants the cheeseburger deluxe platter, with slaw and fries." She popped her eyes open and winked at me. "How'd I do?"

"My order is correct," I said.

"Mine too, although I hate to be so predictable," Jeremy admitted with a rueful grin.

"You know what you like. It's a good thing, in my opinion." Sunny sashayed back to the kitchen.

"Speaking of knowing what you like—" My hands clenched into fists, and my heart pounded in my chest. My molars might've been grinding against each other too. What can I say? I was terrified to get Jeremy's feedback on my book. I'd poured my heart and soul into it.

"What's wrong, Amanda? You look like you're about to pass a kidney stone." Jeremy sipped his iced tea.

I gulped. "I'm anxious about what you have to say about the manuscript. Since you wanted to talk before I read your comments, I'm assuming it's garbage."

He almost did a spit take, as he sputtered and then coughed. "Why would you assume it's garbage?"

"Because you didn't give me any feedback as you read, so I assumed you were just trying to break it to me easy over diner food."

"When have I ever tried to break something to you easy? You know I'm blunt to a fault."

Hope fluttered in my chest. "You mean you didn't hate it?"

"Hate it? I loved it. I mean, sure, I have some notes on places where it needs polishing, but it's an amazing book. I'm so proud of you."

Tears burned in my eyes. "Really?"

"Really. It's why I wanted to meet in person, I wanted to see your face when I told you how good it is." He swept his hand in the air around my face, "Of course, this was not at all how I envisioned it. In my imagination, there was joyous laughter. Perhaps hugging. I didn't think you'd be having an anxiety attack."

"Do you know me at all?"

Jeremy threw back his head and laughed. "You'd think I would after all these years, but you never fail to surprise me."

I slumped against the back of the booth, and took a long sip of my soda. "You have no idea how relieved I am."

We went on to discuss the book until our food came.

As Sunny placed our dishes in front of us, she glanced

toward the entrance and scowled. "Look at what the cat dragged in. I never could stand that girl."

Jeremy had his back to the door. "I don't want to turn around and stare. Who is it?"

"Mallory Davisson," Sunny spit out the name like it was a curse word.

"Ugh, what's she doing back in town?" Jeremy asked.

"If my eyes don't deceive me, she's having dinner with Amanda's man."

This time, Jeremy really did do a spit take.

I YANKED A HANDFUL OF PAPER NAPKINS OUT OF THE dispenser at the end of the booth, next to the little juke box control thingie and shoved them at Jeremy. "Pull it together. They're headed this way."

"But ... but..." He swiped his face.

"I knew about their dinner, and it's nothing to worry about. I'll tell you later," I whispered.

Sunny cocked her head as she listened to us and then turned toward Dylan and Mallory as they approached. "Hello, Dylan. Table or booth?"

"Booth, I think, if that's okay with you?" He glanced at Mallory.

"Whatever you like is fine with me," she flashed a one hundred megawatt smile his way.

"I'll set you up over there," Sunny pointed to a booth a few down from ours. "Sit down when you're ready."

As Sunny bustled off to set up their table, I noticed she'd managed to ignore Mallory completely. Like she wasn't even there. It was unlike Sunny and spoke volumes about the kind of person Mallory was.

"Did you and your little friend decide to have dinner

here to keep an eye on Dylan? How ... sweet." The syrup was so thick, Sunny could've served it over pancakes, but I wasn't fooled. This woman was poison.

Jeremy gasped, and I took a breath to answer before he could lay into her, but Dylan cut us both off by bending down to kiss the top of my head. "Actually, Amanda told me they were having dinner here before she knew we were having our *meeting* here. And I for one, am happy to see her." He smiled at Jeremy. "You too, Jeremy."

"We should get to our booth. Lovely to see you both. Really." Mallory beamed at us before strutting like she was on a catwalk and slid into their booth. Of course taking the seat facing me, which meant Dylan would have his back to me.

"Let the fun begin," he said sotto voce and then followed.

"If insincerity was an Olympic event, Mallory Davisson would get the gold medal every time," Jeremy said. "What's the deal with them? What kind of meeting is it?"

I hesitated, and Jeremy waved his hands for me to continue. "It's very hush-hush right now, so I can't really say. But, it is just a business meeting."

"I could tell that by Dylan's reaction. He is not a happy camper tonight."

He paused and looked at me expectantly, but I shrugged and mimed zipping my lips.

A waitress slid our dinners in front of us. "Anything else I can get you?"

"No thanks, this looks great." My mouth watered at the scent of the bacon on my turkey club.

Once we were alone again, Jeremy reached for the ketchup bottle and said, "Fine. I won't press. But can you at least tell me who she's working for now?"

I pulled a toothpick out of one of the sandwich quarters on my plate. "What happened to not pressing?"

"Hey, I would've asked that about any former schoolmate we ran into. It's not pressing."

"It is a little bit." I bit into my club sandwich, and my eyes fluttered shut.

"Maybe, but you're going to tell me anyway. I mean, I'm not asking about the meeting."

I mulled it over while I chewed and swallowed. "I guess it would be okay. I don't know the name of the company, but she works for Nesbitt Sharpley-Smythe. Have you ever heard of him?"

Jeremy's eyes opened wide. "Of course I've heard of him, he's a real power player in lots of fields." His eyes narrowed, and he frowned at me. "Which, you'll be happy to know, means I learned absolutely nothing about what her meeting with Dylan is."

"Good." I smirked at him. "Anyway, she's evidently a top executive with him. His right-hand person, I think is how she described it."

"Which explains her shoes."

I pointed my sandwich at Jeremy. "Right? I said exactly the same thing."

"They probably cost at least three months of my mortgage payment. I can't help but feel she's up to no good here in Maple Hills."

If he only knew.

~

"ANY COFFEE OR DESSERT?" SUNNY ASKED.

"Lemon meringue pie and a cup of coffee," Jeremy replied without hesitation.

"A cup of decaf for me, please. And an extra fork."

She winked at me. "Goes without saying, where pie is concerned."

As she walked away, Jeremy said, "Did I say I would share my lemon meringue?"

"No, but you always do." There was no shame in my game. We'd been sharing pie at Sunny's and having this same conversation about it since we were at least sixteen years old.

"I didn't want to bring it up while we were eating, but did you hear Dennis Millikan died?"

"Hear about it? I found the body."

"Again? Seriously, you need to find a new hobby. Maybe hiking? Enjoy the fall foliage or something. Although, you'd probably just find someone buried in the forest."

"Trust me, finding his body was not on my agenda for the day. Cara wanted to see the outside of the condo I put the offer on, and there he was." My dinner roiled in my stomach as I remembered touching his cold, stiff hand. I shuddered.

"I wasn't crazy about the guy, but I didn't wish him dead," Jeremy said. "Was it a heart attack?"

"I don't know." Which wasn't a lie, but it also wasn't the complete truth. I wasn't used to keeping anything from Jeremy, and yet there were two things at dinner tonight I didn't feel at liberty to discuss with him, which made this the perfect time to take a little break from our conversation. "I'm going to hit the ladies room before dessert gets here. I'll be right back."

Mallory got up a moment after me, and seemed to be headed the same way. Oh, joy. I couldn't even imagine what girl-talk in the ladies room with that pit viper would be like. She suddenly froze and stared at a man seated at the counter eating a meatloaf platter.

I glanced at him and didn't recognize him. But whoever he was, I figured I could take advantage of Mallory stopping to reach the ladies room and get into a stall before she arrived, to hopefully minimize any conversation with her.

My plan didn't work quite as planned, as I heard the door to the ladies room swing open, just as I was shutting my stall door.

"I know you're in there, Amanda," Mallory's voice called out.

"Hello," I said, but since she couldn't see me, I shook my fist at the door. "Be out in a minute."

It didn't sound as though Mallory used the facilities, and when I emerged from the stall, she stood in front of the mirror reapplying her rosy lip gloss. I stepped up beside her to wash my hands, and she glanced at me in the mirror. Her lip curled up, but her disdain didn't bother me the way it would've in junior high school. Sure, she was gorgeous, and her outfit cost the annual budget of some third-world countries, but my jeans and cute booties were also designer, and much more appropriate for eating at a diner in a small New England town. The tension in my chest eased, as I realized somehow over time, she'd lost her power over me.

"Much as I hate to admit it, I might need your help."

Okay, not what I was expecting to hear. "With what?" I reached for the paper towel dispenser.

"Dylan. Do you think you could use your influence with him to change his mind about the land?" She ground the words out between her teeth.

"Maybe. But I won't. Whatever he decides to do is his business, and I'll support him." I wadded up the paper towels and tossed them in the trash.

Her sapphire blue eyes sparkled in the fluorescent

lighting as she looked at me in the mirror. "It would make him a very wealthy man, and by extension you, if you two stay together."

"I want Dylan to be happy, so like I said, I'll support his decision. Have a nice night, now." I smiled brightly at her. But once the door swung shut behind me, I paused and heaved a deep sigh. She might not have the power to make me feel small anymore, but she was still a deeply unpleasant person. What lengths would she go to for this land deal?

I slid back into the booth and saw an entire piece of pie piled high with fluffy meringue waiting for me. "Thanks for not digging in while I was gone."

"No problem. How were things in there with the dragon lady?" He picked up a fork and dug into the pillowy deliciousness of the mile-high meringue.

"She is a piece of work." As I added creamer to my coffee, I noticed the guy at the lunch counter who'd stopped Mallory in her tracks earlier. He was a nondescript middle-aged guy. Dressed in jeans and a sweatshirt. I jerked my head at him. "Do you know that man?"

Jeremy craned his neck. "Nope. Why?'

"Mallory seemed to recognize him, but I didn't."

"Me neither."

I took a heaping forkful of pie as Sunny approached the table. "Enjoying your meal, kids?"

"Mm-hmm," I managed to get out around a mouthful of lemony, sugary goodness.

"Sunny, do you know the guy seated at the counter?" Jeremy asked.

She looked over. "Probably a leaf peeper. He's staying over at the Dew Drop Inn and has been having a lot of his meals here, but he always pays cash, so I don't know his name. Quiet. Decent tipper. Why do you ask?"

I took a sip of my coffee to wash down the pie. "Neither of us knew him, but it seemed like Mallory might've recognized him."

Speculation gleamed in Sunny's eyes as she glanced between Mallory and the man at the counter. "Really? How odd. Maybe she knows him from New York?"

"Maybe, but they don't look like they go together."

"They do not," Sunny agreed. "So when were you going to tell me you found Dennis Millikan's body this morning?" She raised her voice.

A loud clatter sounded from the counter, where the man had dropped his silverware before turning to look my way. Seeing all of us looking back, he murmured, "Sorry."

"No problem, sugar, let me get you a new fork," Sunny said as she walked behind the counter to help him.

"That was odd," Jeremy said.

"Sure was. He seemed flustered when Sunny mentioned me finding Millikan's body. Doesn't seem like he's your ordinary fall tourist. And what on earth could Mallory Davisson have to do with him?"

Chapter Seven

"What are you doing at the station?"

Fluffy jolted in my arms and yipped, and I jumped at the sound of Danny's voice as I waited for the officer at the desk in the police station to finish a phone call. "Sheesh! Wear a bell, Chief Carlow. You're like a cat."

He chuckled. "How are you doing today, Amanda? Any news on your offer for the condo?"

"We're waiting on the home inspector. He covers a big region, and it could be a couple of weeks before he can look at it." I wrinkled my nose and heaved a sigh.

"Bummer. I know you and The Beast would like your own place." He cast a wary eye at my dog, who in turn was giving him suspicious side-eye. Oh well, baby steps. In the past, she would've snarled at him. "So what are you doing here?"

"I heard from the State Police guy. He wanted me to come in to review my statement, since I'd given it to you and not him."

Danny pursed his lips and narrowed his eyes. "Oh."

Now Fluffy and I both gave him suspicious looks. "What do you mean by that? He said it was routine."

"It probably is. I mean, it makes sense he'd want to talk to you rather than just go by my notes. Especially since you're dating my brother."

"Okay. You made me nervous there."

"It's all new to me too, to tell you the truth. There's not much need to call in the Major Crimes Unit here in sleepy, little Maple Hills."

"May I help you?" The woman behind the plexiglass asked as she hung up the phone.

"Yes. I'm Amanda Seldon, and I'm here to give a statement to the detective from the State Police about Dennis Millikan."

"Right, I'll just let him know you're here." She picked the phone back up and announced me. After putting the receiver back on the cradle, she smiled at me. "He'll be right out."

"No worries. I can bring Amanda back," Danny said.

He opened the locked door leading back to the offices, and gestured for me to go first. I did so, and promptly bumped into a man's chest. "Oops, sorry." I glanced up at him and smiled.

"No problem. Chief Carlow, is this my appointment?" His voice sounded mellow and easy, but a hint of annoyance flashed in his brown eyes.

"It is. We ran into each other in the lobby, and I was bringing her back to you. Amanda Seldon, Detective Evan Panchak." He gestured between us as he made the introduction.

"Thanks for coming in." The overhead light in the hallway gleamed off his shaved head, as he frowned at Fluffy. "I didn't realize you'd be bringing your dog with you."

Danny laughed. A deep, hearty sound. "Aw, you don't need to worry about The Beast. Much."

"Your dog's name is The Beast?"

My lips were in a tight, straight line as I glared at Danny. "No, it's just the chief's idea of a joke. Her name is Fluffy. I hope it's okay I brought her. I'm staying with my parents, and my mom has friends over today, so I couldn't leave her there."

"Because The Beast is so kind and gentle with people she doesn't know," Danny added by way of explanation.

"I guess it's okay. Please keep her under tight control though."

In spite of his attempt to look all easygoing, in his navy polo with the gold state police insignia on the upper left, and khaki trousers, I was picking up a very unyielding vibe from the good detective. I gulped about having to give him my statement. I suspected it was going to be a lot less informal than it had been with Danny at the scene. "Of course."

"See you later, Amanda. Good luck with the home inspection. I hope you don't have to wait too long." Danny waved as he sauntered down the hall to his office.

Detective Panchak opened a door and gestured for me to go inside. My heart rate kicked up a notch when I read the sign on the wall beside it. Interrogation Room. Yeah, this was not going to be a casual recap of finding Dennis Millikan's body.

A table with four office chairs around it was in the middle of the nondescript room. They were the only furnishings, aside from the large mirror on the beige wall behind the side of the table Panchak walked to. I watched enough true crime shows on television to know it was a two-way mirror, and wondered who, if anyone, was on the other side.

He sat down and gestured for me to sit in the seat opposite him. Which put me in full view of the mirror. I glanced nervously at it, while I perched on the chair and clutched Fluffy in my arms. Which, I have to admit, was more to comfort myself than her. I'd been a murder suspect once, and didn't like it one bit. And that time I'd never had to set foot in this terrifying room. The detective opened a manila folder on the table, and ruffled through some papers inside it. I noticed a metal ring bolted to the table, and again my reality TV addiction told me it was for handcuffing prisoners, so they couldn't make a run for it.

Fluffy must've picked up on my tension, because her ears flattened against her head and she growled softly at Panchak.

"Shh ... it's okay, Fluff," I murmured in a soothing tone as I stroked her tense back. You and me both, little buddy. I wish someone was here to rub my tight shoulders. This room was awful. I was ready to confess to jaywalking last week.

Panchak smiled across the table at me in a way clearly designed to set me at ease. It didn't work.

"I've read the statement you gave Chief Carlow on the scene, but I'd like to hear it from you directly. Especially in light of information that has arisen about the cause of death."

"Has it been determined?"

He nodded; his eyes flinty. "It has, and it was poison."

I gasped. "Poison?" My suspicions about the apple and bottle of cider next to the body seemed to have been correct. An apple and cider from Dylan's orchard. My anxiety about this interview just went up to eleven on a scale of one to ten.

He placed a tiny recorder out on the table. "Just for my records. More accurate than taking notes."

I swallowed hard and nodded, and was ready to add to my jaywalking confession about the time I only waited a bare second at a stop sign, rather than the required three seconds, before I drove through the intersection. I'm a surprisingly law-abiding citizen for someone who's been questioned in two murder cases in the past three months. What can I say? Jaywalking and a rolling stop through an empty intersection are my biggest infractions.

"Why don't you tell me about that morning," he prompted with another warm smile, which didn't quite reach his eyes.

He maintained eye contact with me the whole time I recounted my story of finding Millikan's body yesterday morning. When I was done, he said, "Very good, thanks. But let's back up a little bit now, where were you the night before?"

I scrunched up my nose. "The night before I found the body?"

"Correct."

"I had dinner at my boyfriend's house, and then went back to my parents' house, where I'm living right now."

Paper crinkled as he reviewed notes from the file. He pointed to a sheet of paper. "And your boyfriend is Dylan Carlow, correct?"

"Yes." Again, from true crime television and podcasts, I knew not to volunteer more information than was asked.

"What time did you leave Mr. Carlow's home?"

"Around ten o'clock."

"And you went straight home at that time?"

"I did."

He smiled and nodded at me to continue. I did not.

After an uncomfortably long pause, the smile faded at the edges of his lips, and he cleared his throat. "And Mr. Carlow remained at his home?"

"Yes."

Another long silence and when I added nothing, he asked, "And he remained there all night to the best of your knowledge?"

"Yes."

This time he didn't even bother with the good old boy grin. Muscles worked in his cheeks, and I thought all that grinding couldn't be good for his teeth. "Did he have plans to go out after you left? Perhaps to meet with Mr. Millikan?"

A fine sheen of sweat formed at my hairline. This man was suspicious of Dylan, and it was obvious to me this meeting wasn't merely a chance to hear my statement live and in person. "I've got to be honest with you, Detective Panchak... "

He leaned forward in his chair. "You can tell me anything, Ms. Seldon."

"Then I have to tell you, this interview is starting to feel a lot more like an interrogation than a witness statement, and I'm not at all comfortable with it. Do I need to contact an attorney?"

He sat back in his seat, and I could practically hear his teeth grinding this time. I jumped as my phone buzzed loudly from my purse on the chair next to mine. "Excuse me." I held Fluffy in place with one hand and dug my phone out of my oversized handbag with the other. I glanced at it and happy excitement took over from the anxious tension of this meeting. "It's a text from my real estate agent. The home inspector had a cancellation and can look at my condo this afternoon."

"Yes?" His brows met in the middle of his eyes.

"If I don't take this appointment, I'll have to wait weeks. I'll need to end our meeting now, Detective. I'm sorry." *Spoiler alert, I totally wasn't.*

He chuffed out a breath. "Fine. I'll be in touch if I need to speak to you again. Please don't leave town, Ms. Seldon."

His tone was fairly amiable, but the threat was clear. I rose and slung my bag over one shoulder, and Fluffy's whiskers twitched as she stared at him through narrowed eyes. I attempted to keep my tone light and breezy too, but the snark was strong in me when I said, "Where would I go, Detective?"

~

I GLANCED DOWN THE HALL TOWARD DANNY'S OFFICE, BUT the door was shut. Probably better if I didn't leave the interrogation room to go straight to the chief's office anyway. I hustled out of the police station as quickly as I could without it looking like I was literally running away.

When I emerged onto the sidewalk, I stopped, put Fluffy down on the concrete, and inhaled a deep breath of crisp, autumn air.

"Are you okay, Mandy-bel?"

I jumped at the sound of Aunt Lori's voice from the sidewalk to my right. The meeting had shaken me up more than I wanted to admit. How could Detective Panchak think Dylan could kill anyone?

"I guess not." She reached out and rubbed my shoulder and then winced, "What do you have under your sweater? Rocks? You're so stressed. Tell me what's going on."

"I just had a meeting with a state police detective about Dennis Millikan. It was supposed to be a simple recap of my earlier statement to Danny, but somewhere along the line it turned into a full-on interrogation." I glanced around to be sure no one was close by and added in a whisper, "I think he suspects Dylan."

"What? That's nuts!"

"Tell me about it. I even asked him if I needed an attorney present."

"And did you?"

I shrugged. "He didn't get a chance to answer me. I got a text from my real estate agent. The inspector can look at the condo right now, so I explained and rushed out. He told me not to leave town."

Her eyes opened wide. "Where would you go?"

"That's what I said!" We both chuckled, and the tension eased in my chest now I was out of the dreary interrogation room.

"Was it the good looking state police detective I've been seeing around town?" Aunt Lori asked. "I'm sorry to hear he's a jerk."

"He wasn't bad looking, I guess. I was too busy being terrified of him to notice. And I don't think he's a jerk. Just mistaken about Dylan."

"I'm glad to hear it, because he is attractive, in a commanding sort of way."

"Like a dictator, you mean?" I joked. "No, seriously, he probably is a nice guy, but I'd guess he's about my age."

She raised one shoulder delicately and let it drop. "Are you implying he's a little young for me? If I were a man and he were a woman, no one would think twice about the age difference."

I bobbed my head. "You have a good point. Just do me a favor if you do go out with him. Please convince him Dylan couldn't harm a fly."

"You got it. So, where are you headed now?"

"I've got to get over to the condo and meet my agent and the inspector. How about you?"

"I'm actually off this afternoon, so would you mind if I tagged along? I've been dying to see your condo."

"I'd love it! Can you come right now?"

She jerked her head back toward the library. "Let me just run back and grab some books for Lynn Prattleworth. She lives at the Lakeshore Condos, and this will save her a trip into town. I know she doesn't like to drive too much anymore."

"That's nice of you. Let me grab my car, and I'll meet you in front of the library in a few."

She nodded and trotted back toward the brick library building. I picked up Fluffy to carry her, even though she was perfectly capable of walking under her own steam. The problem was, we were in a hurry, and Fluff would want to sniff every lamppost between here and the municipal parking lot next to the town green.

I picked up the pace, glad to be walking out of the police station a free woman, and to not have implicated Dylan in any way. I paused and waited for the light to change to cross Main Street, and wondered if it would be acceptable for me to talk to Danny about what happened in the interrogation room. I imagined if he'd been taken off the case, he wouldn't have been the person on the other side of the two-way mirror.

The walk sign flashed, and I scurried across the street. I needed to let Dylan know the direction this questioning had gone, so he'd be prepared. Was there some way to let Panchak know just how very many people in town had beefed with Millikan, without it looking like I was trying to cast suspicion away from my boyfriend?

Chapter Eight

"I'll contact you when I have news, doll. But the inspection couldn't have gone better." My agent grinned devilishly and pointed at Aunt Lori. "And I'll see *you* for happy hour at Hitchcock's next week."

"You're on," Lori replied.

Evelyn climbed up into her massive SUV and pulled off with a cheery toot of the horn.

"I think I almost own a condo." I held up crossed fingers on both hands.

"No doubt." Aunt Lori peered at someone a few condos down. She waved at a short, round lady walking a massive dog. "Hello! Lynn, I brought your library books. Let me grab them from my niece's car, and I'll be right there."

"Thanks, Lori. I really appreciate it. I'll come to you though, we're out for our afternoon walk anyway."

I popped the trunk of my car so Aunt Lori could retrieve the books. She whispered out the side of her mouth, "Afternoon walk, my Aunt Fanny. She's coming down here to snoop. Lynn Prattleworth never misses a trick."

Fluffy tugged at the end of her leash, barking ferociously at the approaching dog. A gutsy move since she was roughly the size of his big, square head. Luckily, the other dog's gentle bemusement indicated he had no ax to grind with my Fluff. He even wagged his tail tentatively.

"Stop it, girl. Be nice. You're picking a fight out of your weight class." I raised my voice to be heard above her barking.

"It's all right, Brutus is a lover, not a fighter." Lynn chuckled and tucked a stray hair from her longish, gray pixie cut behind her ear.

Realizing no one was going to engage with her, Fluffy's barks faded to a half-hearted growl, which quickly faded altogether. She took a step toward Brutus and sniffed. He put his head down and sniffed her as well, and it soon became clear they'd be friends. Dog fight crisis averted. Which was good news for Brutus, as the big, brindle dog would've fared worse than my girl in their matchup.

"I'm Lynn Prattleworth. Are you buying number fourteen?"

"Amanda Seldon, and yes I am. Hopefully. We just had the inspection. And this is Fluffy."

Lori handed her the library tote bag of books. "Here you go."

"Thank you so much. If you can wait a minute, I'll run these home and bring back your bag."

"Don't bother. You can just return them in it." She put her hands on her hips and looked around. "I'm excited my niece is going to be living here. It's a beautiful spot."

"It certainly is. When my darling Abner passed, I rattled around in our big house. It was a hard decision to sell the home we shared, but I've been much happier here. And there's always something to see, and someone to talk to."

"Which is lovely." Aunt Lori's tone betrayed nothing but kindliness, but I saw the distinct twinkle in her eyes when she looked at me. "I think it's going to be a great place for Amanda and Fluffy."

I appreciated the fact she hadn't called me "Mandy-bel" in front of this woman.

"Of course, you could probably get unit sixteen for a song, since that obnoxious Dennis Millikan went and got himself killed there." She pursed her lips.

"I only met him a couple of times ... well, when he was alive. But both times he was arguing with people," I said.

She turned her bright-eyed gaze my way. "When he was alive? That's right. You're the one who found the body. I heard it was the person who was buying fourteen. It must have been awful for you."

"It wasn't the best morning I ever had." Of course, I didn't feel the need to bring up the fact there was another morning in the not-so-distant past when I'd also found a murdered body. No need to scare the neighbors.

"The State Police Major Crimes Unit van was here for hours investigating, which was my first clue he didn't just drop dead of a heart attack or something. A very attractive young detective even came over to talk to me."

"Was his name Panchak?" I asked.

"Yes. How did you know?"

"I met with him this morning. He wanted to get my statement about finding the body."

Aunt Lori swatted my arm, "See, I told you he was a cutie."

Lynn waggled her eyebrows at me. "This one has her

own handsome young man, from what I've heard around town. Dylan Carlow. Quite a catch, so you can't blame her for not noticing Detective Panchak's good looks."

"What did he talk to you about?" I asked.

"He wanted to know if I'd seen anyone around Dennis's place. Anything unusual. Which, of course, I had."

Aunt Lori gasped. "Really? What did you see?"

"The afternoon of the night he died, Dennis came home from Maple Hills Orchard. I could tell, because he had a bag of apples from there and a six-pack of their delicious new cider. Anyway, there was a man waiting in a car for him. It had Illinois plates, so I knew he was an out-of-towner."

"And he was waiting for Millikan?" I asked.

"Yes, as soon as Dennis got out of his car, this man jumped out of his, and the two of them fought like cats and dogs. I couldn't hear what they were saying, but their faces were both as red as your car." She gestured toward my sedan. "And they got right up in each other's grill, as the young people say."

I fought against a bubble of laughter at the elderly lady's use of slang, but I mustn't have done a very good job, because she pointed to me and chuckled. "I see you're surprised, but I've got grandchildren. I know what's what in the world. You gotta keep current with the lingo, y'know?"

Aunt Lori patted her arm. "It's important to roll with the times, I agree. So, what happened next with Dennis and the stranger? Did they come to blows?"

She shook her head. "Nope. Just lots of yelling. Then Dennis stormed into his condo and slammed the door in the other man's face. He pounded on the door for a bit, and finally Dennis opened it and let him inside. Neither of them looked happy though, and then I couldn't see what happened. But next time I looked outside, his car was gone."

"Hmm ... so the police know about this man?" I asked.

"Oh, yes. I told the hunky detective all about him. He was very interested. But I'm sorry to say, he was more interested to hear Dennis had the apples and cider from Dylan's orchard." She looked my way with a sympathetic moue. "Sorry, Amanda. I didn't mean to throw Dylan under the bus. I just told the him what I saw, but Detective Panchak found it very interesting Dennis came home with those particular items from the Orchard on the day he died.

Well, crud. It seemed as though even with a prime suspect in the out-of-towner, Panchak was bound and determined to focus his investigation on Dylan.

THE NEXT DAY WAS ONE OF THOSE BRIGHT OCTOBER DAYS in Maple Hills, where the temperature was chilly in the morning, but the sun warmed it up to a comfortable seventy as the day progressed.

I decided to take advantage of the gorgeous weather before the cold set in for the next several months. I packed up my laptop and Fluffy and headed to the Sit and Sip, to get a coffee and review Jeremy's edits at one of their outdoor café tables. With Fluffy's leash looped around my chair, she settled in under the table and rested her chin on my feet.

Immersed in my work, time passed in a flash, and I was surprised when I picked up my coffee to take a sip and realized it was empty.

"If it isn't my favorite former chambermaid." A raspy woman's voice called out from the sidewalk.

I looked up to see an older lady with a tight, gray perm striding toward me. Fluffy stood up and planted herself solidly in front of me. Her tail down and hackles raised. "Down, Fluff. It's Carol Godfrey. You know her. She's our friend."

"Glad to hear I'm your friend. I hope The Beast believes it." She laughed so hard at her own joke she wheezed.

"She does. I mean, anyone who thought I was a good chambermaid the summer I worked at the Dew Drop Inn has to be our friend."

"I was actually being kind. You were the worst! But you tried really hard, and I've always had a soft spot for you. Are you busy writing, or do you mind if I take a load off and we can catch up?" She gestured to the empty seat at my table.

"I was just about to take a break, so please, sit."

She flopped into the seat with a grunt. "How's the book coming?"

"Good. I've finished the first draft, and Jeremy edited it. I'm reviewing his comments now. Pretty soon, I'll be ready to publish."

"And how does that work?"

"I'm still researching and learning all my options, but right now I'm leaning toward publishing it independently."

"What do you mean?" She scratched her head.

"I would do it myself, without a publishing company. Hire my own cover designer, editor, format it myself."

"Sounds like a lot of work."

"It would be, but I'd have more control over the whole process, which I like." Okay, some of my former employees might've referred to me as a control freak, but I knew if I did something myself it was done just how I liked it. "And more importantly, if I publish it myself, I can potentially start earning money faster. And a little income wouldn't be amiss."

"And you wouldn't have to split it with a publishing company?" Carol asked.

"Right. Another benefit."

"Sounds like an excellent plan then. Good luck."

"Thanks, I'll take all the good luck I can get, because I'm starting from scratch here knowledge-wise."

"You're a sharp cookie. I have every faith you'll be a success."

"Aww, I appreciate it. So how are things going at the Dew Drop?"

She chuffed out a breath. "Busy, busy, busy. I swear, every year we have more leaf peepers coming up here. But it's good for business, so I shouldn't complain. You've been working at the Maple Hills Orchard, right?"

"In the seasonal shop, yes. And we've been slammed there too. It's like people have never seen an apple before."

"Speaking of apples," Carol narrowed her eyes and peered at me. "I hear you found another dead body. That Millikan blowhard. And there was a Maple Hills Orchard hard cider by his side."

"Word sure spreads fast."

"With Lynn Prattleworth living next door to the scene of the crime?" She shrugged. "Everyone knew pretty fast. But, I want you to know I don't believe the rumors about Dylan Carlow whacking him with poisoned cider for a minute."

My heart thudded. "Thanks. Dylan most certainly did not kill him, so whatever you can do to help spread the word around town, I'd appreciate it."

"On it like a bonnet."

"I hope they find the real killer fast, so the rumors about Dylan go away, and people forget all about them." I sat up straighter and cocked my head. "Speaking of the real killer, I wanted to ask you if you had a middle-aged guy staying at the Dew Drop. His car has Illinois plates."

"Sure do. His name is Gary Bullaro. He's been a guest for a few days now. Kind of funny though, he's all by himself, and I don't really know what he's doing here. I don't think he's in town for the foliage." She clasped her hands over her heart. "Wait a gosh darned minute. What do you mean by 'speaking of the real killer'? Do you think Mr. Bullaro might be a murderer? And he's staying at my place."

"I don't know if he's a killer, but Lynn Prattleworth saw him waiting for Millikan to get home the day he died and then arguing with him in the parking lot at the condo. I just wanted to learn a little bit more about him."

"Sorry, kiddo. I don't know anything about him. He keeps to himself. But I'll sure as heck keep an eye on him."

"I saw a guy at the diner the other night. I wonder if he's the same person. Salt-and-pepper hair, barrel-chested, middle-aged?"

"That sounds like him."

Interesting. Because Mallory Davisson had clearly recognized the man, and was startled to see him. Which begs the question, what on earth could Mallory Davisson have to do with a middle-aged man from Illinois, who fought with Millikan the day he was murdered?

I struggled to concentrate after Carol went on her way, hopefully to spread the word of Dylan's innocence far and wide. My mind hummed with thoughts of Millikan's death, and who might've done the man in and also wanted to throw suspicion on my boyfriend.

My phone buzzed and vibrated on the table next to my laptop. I saw it was a call from Aunt Lori.

"How's my favorite aunt?"

"Just fine. How's my favorite niece?"

"Bothered by this murder. I think I figured out who the guy Lynn Prattleworth told us about is. He's staying at the Dew Drop."

"Interesting. Speaking of Lynn, she's the reason I wanted to talk to you. She just called the library. She said she remembered something else about the day Millikan was killed."

"Something not involving Dylan, I sincerely hope."

"Of course not. She said she saw Bitsy Van Dyke's car in the lot after he had the fight with the out-of-towner."

My eyebrows shot skyward. "Bitsy? She hated Millikan with a white-hot passion."

"I know. She blames him for Adrian's accident and subsequent issues. So, what was she doing at his condo on the day he died?"

"I don't know, but I'd sure like to find out," I said fervently.

"Then let your favorite aunt do you a favor."

I chuckled, because she was actually my only aunt, and I was her only niece. It was a running joke we had. "What kind of favor? You're making it sound like some sort of deal with the mob."

Lori's deep, throaty laugh sounded through the phone. "Nothing that bad. My property tax is due, and I'm tied up at the library until this evening. I was wondering if you'd want to swing by to get my check and take it to Town Hall for me?"

"That sounds more like a favor to you than to me."

"You forget, Bitsy Van Dyke works at Town Hall, and is actually the person you'd need to deliver my check to."

"You really are my favorite aunt, you know. I'll be at the library in five minutes."

Chapter Nine

"I got here as fast—" I skidded into Aunt Lori's office with my laptop tote slung over one shoulder and clutching Fluffy with my other arm. My words died on my lips when I saw she was on the phone. "Sorry," I mouthed and lowered myself into a guest chair across the desk from her.

"She just got here, Bitsy, so she should be at Town Hall in a little bit. Oh, and one other thing, she has Fluffy with her. Will that be okay?"

I picked up one of Fluffy's paws and waved it at my aunt, who bit back a smile and rolled her eyes at me.

"It's okay with you? Thanks so much, Bitsy." She paused and listened to the woman on the other end of the call. "Sounds good. See you soon. Bye."

She slumped down in her chair. "That woman is so dithering. She makes me weary. And now I've contacted her, she wants to get together for lunch. Like we're besties or something. The things I do for your sleuthing."

"Like dating a millionaire Broadway producer?" I opened my eyes in innocence, but my tongue was firmly in my cheek, as I reminded her of the so-called sacrifice she made for a case last summer.

"All right, I concede it was no hardship. But an entire meal with Bitsy Van Dyke? Dylan and Hitch owe me."

I furrowed my brow. "Hitch? What does Hitch have to do with the murder?"

"That detective came by to see me earlier today. He'd heard about the argument Hitch had with Dennis at Hitchcock's the other night and was asking me very probing questions. As if Hitch would ever harm a fly." She scowled.

"Not thinking Detective Panchak is such a cutie now you've been on the receiving end of one of his interrogations, are you?"

"He's still hot, but I have lost all interest in him. I must be evolving, because I'm discovering I need more than a smoking hot young man to catch my interest. Like a sense of humor."

"One area where Evan Panchak is distinctly lacking." I bobbed my head.

"He even said he heard I'd spoken sharply to Dennis. I told him I would never poison someone. If I wanted to kill them, it would be face-to-face with a knife, so they would know it was me."

I snorted. "And what did he have to say to that revelation?"

One side of her mouth quirked up, and merriment danced in her eyes. "He seemed uncomfortable with me after I let that little conversational bomb drop."

Fluffy bounced on my lap as my stomach shook with laughter. I gasped out a breath and said, "You better sincerely hope no one gets stabbed here in town, or you're going to be Public Enemy Number One."

"Do me a favor, and find the real killer so Panchak stops barking up the wrong apple trees."

I tapped my hand to my head in a mock salute. "I'm on it, ma'am. Please don't stab me."

I FOLLOWED THE SIGNS IN TOWN HALL TO FIND THE OFFICE to pay property taxes. Luckily, it was deserted at this time of day, so no one complained about me having a dog with me. I squinted at the sign next to an open door. This was the place, and a quick peek inside told me Bitsy was there and waiting.

"Hi, Ms. Van Dyke. Thank you for letting me bring Fluffy with me. Which reminds me, I need to get her Maple Hills dog license too, but I can come back another day to do it. I know it's late in the day, but Aunt Lori was very anxious for me to get this check to you before the end of business." I rooted around in my tote bag for the check and held Fluffy with one arm.

"Please, call me Bitsy. Come back any time during business hours for this cutie-pie's license. And bringing her today is no problem at all. I like dogs. Well, an animal lover of all sorts really. Although, I don't have any pets right now. My son wants to get a dog, but a cat might be better. Y'know they need less attention. Maybe a bird. Or a hamster? But right now, my son takes all of my care and attention, so there's nothing left for an animal. And if you're going to have a pet, I really think it's a big responsibility, and you owe it to the creature to give it your all." She paused from her lengthy, tittering monologue to suck in a deep breath.

Phew. I could see what Aunt Lori meant about Bitsy making her weary.

Before she could wind up to say anymore, I waved the check triumphantly in the air. "Found it! Here you go, Bitsy."

She took it from my hand, and began to click on the computer in front of her. "Thank you so much. It's nice of you to help your aunt. Family is everything, really, isn't it? But you'd know that. You came back to town after your father's open-heart surgery, and I know it must have been such a blessing to your parents. Having an ill family member is so difficult—"

"You'd know all about those difficulties, after your son's accident." I interrupted again, in an attempt to steer the conversation away from me and onto Bitsy.

She blinked against tears in her eyes, and her voice quavered more than usual. "You have no idea. To see your child permanently changed, suffering, struggling. And all because of the thoughtless, selfish actions of one man." Bitsy took a tissue from the box and dabbed at her eyes.

"Dennis Millikan, you mean?" I prompted.

"That monster. Yes, he's who I mean. Did you know him?"

I shook my head. "Not really. I ran into him around town a couple of times, and he always seemed to be fighting with one person or another." I paused and added in a gentle tone, "Including you."

The light of recognition shone in her eyes, and she held her hands over her heart. "That's right. You were at Hitchcock's Tavern the night he was so cruel to me. And after what he did to my Adrian. He was always such a good boy, until he discovered Oh Denny Boy's micro-brewery."

"I'm so sorry. I have to admit, I don't really know what happened."

"He was home for the summer from college, and he

went to Millikan's bar. Not a lot of locals go there, but the younger people seem to like it. I guess their parents are at Hitchcock's, so they want to go somewhere else. The night of the accident, his blood alcohol level was well above the legal limit. Millikan should never have continued to serve him, but Adrian told me afterwards he just kept pouring the beers, offering free shots of tequila. And when it came time for him to leave, Adrian could barely walk. Hitch would never let someone leave his establishment on their own in that condition. But Millikan didn't even try to get him to call a cab, or a friend, or a ride share. He just let him leave. My baby. And he hit a tree." The effort of getting the story out in one breath the way she talked was too much for her, and she slumped in the chair, shoulders shaking. From anger or grief I couldn't tell.

"How horrible, Bitsy. I'm so sorry. I can understand why you hate him so much."

She snuffled into her tissue, but rage flashed in her eyes. "I do hate him. A hatred deeper than I ever dreamed I would be capable of holding in my heart. I'm glad he's dead. Glad."

I went from thinking Bitsy was a slightly ditzy older woman, to a woman who might have been furious enough at Millikan to have plotted his death.

But she did leave me an opening. "What I don't under-stand, Bitsy, is since you hated him so much, what were you doing at his condo the day he died?"

Bitsy's eyebrows met in the middle of her face, and she frowned. "What are you talking about?"

"Your car was seen parked there."

She pursed her lips. "By Lynn Prattleworth, I'd wager. She is such a busybody."

Not wanting to throw my potential new neighbor

under the bus, I shrugged. "It was just something I heard around town."

"Well, I wasn't there—" She abruptly stopped talking, and silence was not Bitsy Van Dyke's natural state. Her gaze darted from side to side and she rushed to fill the silence, "Lori's taxes are all set now, so you should probably be on your way. I'm breaking the rules by allowing you to have your dog here, and I can't afford to lose this job and my insurance. Without it, I could never afford Adrian's medical bills."

"Of course, we'll be on our way. I didn't mean to get you into trouble at work."

"Buh-bye." Bitsy waggled her fingers at me and pointedly went back to typing on her computer.

"Bye," I murmured as Fluffy and I beat a hasty retreat.

The footsteps of my cute booties echoed in the empty hallway as we walked away from Bitsy's office. We managed to get out of the building without running into anyone else, so Bitsy's job should be safe.

Once in the parking lot, I looked down at Fluffy. "What made her give us the bum's rush? Was she really afraid of getting fired for allowing you in her office? Or was she panicked to learn her car had been spotted at Millikan's?"

Fluffy had no answer for me.

As Dylan washed the dinner dishes and I dried, I recounted my conversation with Bitsy.

"She was obsessed with Millikan. Maybe she used to do surveillance on his place or something, and was embarrassed someone had seen her spying." He handed me the pasta pot.

"Sounds like stalking to me, and it's still wacky." I dried the pot with a white dish towel with, what else, a red apple on it.

Since the pot was the last item to wash, Dylan dried his hands on another apple towel. "No, but Adrian really was messed up after the wreck. I don't necessarily agree with her about it being 100 percent Millikan's fault. He wasn't pouring the drinks down Adrian's throat. And he was twenty-one at the time. She views him as her baby, and treats him like one too. But he is above legal age."

A knock sounded at the kitchen door.

Dylan flipped on the back porch lights to reveal his brother. He threw open the door. "Hey, Danny. What are you doing here? Is everything all right."

Dressed in jeans and a sweatshirt, Danny looked younger and less formidable than he did in his police chief uniform. I waved the dish towel at him before drying my hands with it. "Hi, Danny."

"Hi, guys, nothing is wrong. Rita is at her book club tonight, and the girls are out too, an away field hockey game for Sophie, and Bella is at a friend's house. I stopped by to see how you're doing."

"I'm okay." Dylan shrugged. "Can't say I love being a murder suspect, but I know you can't talk about the case, so we won't."

Danny squeezed his brother's shoulder. "I know, man. I'm sorry. I wish there was something I can do. Evan is a good detective, so we just have to keep the faith he'll get to the right conclusion eventually."

"We were just about to go to the diner for dessert, do you want to come with?" I asked.

He cocked his head. "The diner for dessert, when I see an apple cake on the counter?"

"I just really want something non-apple based for dessert tonight." Dylan grinned. "Amanda's mom made the cake for me, and it's great, but with just one or two people eating it, it's lasting forever. We were thinking lemon meringue pie at Sunny's would do the trick tonight. Plus, y'know, I'm trying not to scare Amanda away with apple overexposure."

"This point in the season *is* apple overload. Sure, I'll go with you guys. As long as you don't mind me tagging along?"

"Not at all," I said.

"Nope," Dylan said at the exact same time, and we all laughed.

"I'll take my own car, because I'm going to have to pick up Bella in about an hour."

"THIS PLACE IS JUMPING TONIGHT. I BET DANNY'S SORRY HE brought his car too." I scanned Sunny Side Up's parking lot for an empty space. I bounced in my seat and pointed. "Ooo! That car's brake lights are on, maybe they're leaving."

Sure enough, they were, and we snagged the spot.

As we strolled toward the entrance, Dylan looked around with a frown on his face. "Do you see Danny's car?"

Before I could answer, Danny called out from the sidewalk. "Hey guys, hold up. I decided to just park on the street. I hope we can get seats in here. This is crazy."

We waited for him and then walked into the diner together. The hostess stand was empty, and I caught a glimpse of Sunny seating some people at a table in the center of the restaurant. Her hair was disheveled and even bigger than usual. She spotted me and waved, before bustling back toward us.

"I'm sorry, but I seated them at the last table, kids. Is the counter all right?" She asked, her usual smile nowhere to be seen.

"Sure," Dylan said immediately.

"No problem, we're just here for some dessert without apples. Trying to shield Amanda from the apple-centric nature of the Carlow family." Danny winked at Sunny, which teased a smile to her face.

"Non-apple desserts we got. Although most of the people here are leaf peepers, so they want apple and maple on everything. And don't even get me started on pumpkin spice." She rolled her eyes dramatically, grabbed three menus and waved over her shoulder for us to follow.

She pointed to three empty seats together at the counter and scooted behind it to hand us our menus.

Danny sat in the one on the far left, Dylan next to him, and I took the one next to Dylan. As I slid onto my stainless steel stool with its padded, red seat, I glanced at the man seated on my right. My pulse did a little samba as I realized it was the mystery man from Illinois. The one who'd been seen arguing with Dennis Millikan outside his condo on the afternoon of his death. Maybe this was my chance to learn a little bit more about him.

As Sunny handed me an oversized menu, she continued talking right from where she left off before seating us. "Since they renovated the Maple Hills Arms, and turned it into a fancy-schmancy boutique hotel, our little town has become a prime autumn tourist destination. They have no vacancies, and neither does the Dew Drop. It's getting all their overflow guests."

The Dew Drop Inn was an old-fashioned motel, built in the middle of the last century, and looked it. One story, with rooms opening onto the parking lot, and neon. Lots of neon. But it did have an excellent location right on the lake, and now that I was no longer a chambermaid there, the rooms were clean and comfortable.

"Not quite the same level of accommodations," Dylan said as if he'd read my mind.

"No, but they're out and about all day, so it's all right. The orchard must be slammed right now too, huh?" Sunny asked as she poured us each a glass of water.

"It is rocking," Dylan said. "Sales are already ahead of the entire month last October. But I can't complain."

"Me either," Sunny said with alacrity, but then flashed a roguish smile at us. "But I can't say I won't be sorry when January rolls around. I'm thinking I might go for a week to one of those all-inclusive resorts in the Caribbean, and be a tourist myself for a change. See how the other half lives." She glanced at the door. "More customers just arrived. I'll be back for your order in a bit."

While she rushed off, I swung on my stool and smiled at the man next to me. "Are you in town for the fall foliage?"

He started and slanted a glance at me. "Nope. Although it is pretty scenery here."

I took a sip of my water. "What brings you to Maple Hills then? Not much here for tourists aside from the beautiful autumn scenery. My name's Amanda Seldon, by the way."

Dylan leaned forward and looked to his right to see who I was talking to. He flashed a quizzical glance my way, before Danny mentioned the baseball playoffs and the two of them started to chat about sports.

"Uh, I'm Gary. Gary Bullaro, and I came here on business."

"So you're here for business. I hope it went well." I

kept my voice bright, and I crossed my fingers I sounded more innocent to him than I did to myself.

He shrugged and took a sip of his beer. "It did not."

"Oh, I'm so sorry." His terse words didn't encourage continued conversation, but nothing ventured, nothing gained where sleuthing was concerned, so I forged ahead. "Not much business here in our little town. What do you do?"

There was a long pause when I thought he wouldn't answer, and I crossed my fingers. Dylan and Danny had stopped talking and both glanced down the counter at us. I knew they had to be wondering why I was talking to a stranger, especially one who clearly did not want to be talking to me.

Finally, Gary answered. "I used to be a co-owner of a microbrewery back in Illinois. With the person I came here to see. Back before he screwed me over and sold out our business."

"You must be talking about Dennis Millikan," I said.

He narrowed his eyes. "You knew him?"

I shrugged and kept my voice casual. "I met him once or twice, but he seemed like he wasn't the nicest person, and I know he owned a new microbrewery here in town—"

"Oh Denny Boy's," Gary said with a snort of derision. "It was my idea. All of it. He took it and sold out to a rich investor behind my back. I came here to try to get my fair share."

"But I guess he didn't agree, since you said the meeting didn't go well."

"He did not. And then I didn't get the chance to talk to him again, because he up and died on me. A pain in my a —I mean pain in my neck, up until the end."

Gary didn't exactly seem heartbroken about Millikan's

death, but it didn't appear to benefit him in any way either. Unless... "Maybe you could meet with his rich investor yourself now. Do you know who it was?"

"Sure do, Nesbitt Sharpley-Smythe. And I spotted his second-in-command in town this week. Maybe I'll talk to her."

"Is that Mallory Davisson?" I asked, trying to keep the excitement out of my voice. If so, it might explain how she recognized Gary at the diner the other night.

"Yeah. Do you know her?"

"Maple Hills is her hometown. We went to high school together."

"Going into business with Sharpley-Smythe would be like crawling into bed with the devil, but like the devil himself, he's got a lot of money. Why shouldn't some of it come my way, when Oh Denny Boy's was my brainchild all along? All Dennis had was the name."

Mallory had been surprised to see Gary, and not in a happy way, so I suspected she wouldn't be interested in doing business with him, but who knows? What really interested me was the fact there was now a connection between the murdered man and Mallory and her boss. I didn't like the woman, but I didn't want to believe she could be the one who killed Millikan.

Chapter Ten

"That was an interesting observation about Mallory and her employer." Danny's breath came out as puffs of steam in the chilly, October night air.

"Sure was," Dylan agreed.

"Confirmed for me our family made the right decision by turning down their offer for our land."

Harp music came out of Danny's pants. No, really. "You got angels down your drawers?" Dylan asked with a grin.

Danny playfully punched his brother's bicep and pulled his phone out of his pocket. "It's Bella's ringtone." He peered at the screen. "And she's ready for her chauffeur to pick her up and drive her home, sorry to cut this short."

"No worries. My mom is in the same book club as Rita, so I left Dad alone with Fluffy. I should be getting home too."

"I hope you don't find The Beast feasting on his bones when you get home." Danny shuddered.

"That's not fair, she's getting better," I defended my little furry buddy.

"True," Dylan chimed in. "Last time Fluffy saw you, she barely even growled."

I think I would've loved him, just for his affection for my prickly dog alone, even without all his other positive attributes. Warmth spread outward from my heart, and even on a brisk New England evening, I felt toasty.

Danny snickered. "Yeah, it was a beautiful moment. See you guys around. Thanks for letting me crash your non-apple party."

We said our goodbyes, and Danny jogged up the street to where he'd parked his car. I rubbed my hands together and regretted I didn't have gloves with me, but southern California weather had spoiled me, and it never even occurred to me to bring a pair tonight. I took a step toward Dylan's truck, and was stopped by his voice behind me.

"Danny chose to ignore the fact you were clearly pumping that guy for information about Millikan's murder, maybe so he wouldn't be complicit if your sleuthing came to light. Possibly so he wouldn't have to rat you out to the state police. But I'm not going to pretend I didn't see you going all reckless and Nancy Drew in there." He pulled out his key fob and unlocked the truck, as he walked toward it.

I fell in step beside him. "Nancy Drew I'll give you. But, reckless? As far as Gary Bullaro was concerned, I was just a local chatting with a tourist at the diner counter. Nothing too death-defying there. I was even with the police chief."

We'd reached the truck and stopped behind the back of it.

Dylan shook his head. "Unless of course Bullaro is the killer, and he finds out what you were up to. Have you already forgotten about last summer? The way the murderer tried to make you their second victim?"

He didn't wait for an answer and opened the passenger

side door for me. As he helped me climb into the cab of the big truck, I said, "I most certainly have not forgotten about someone trying to kill me. I don't think I ever will." I turned my head to look him straight in the eye where he stood at the door of the truck. "But do you remember you're Detective Panchak's prime suspect in Millikan's murder?"

"I do." Dylan stepped back and closed the truck door before skirting around the front of the vehicle and getting into the driver's seat, where he continued his sentence. "But I don't want you getting yourself killed trying to clear my name."

Dylan started the truck and carefully backed out of the tight parking space. Not wanting to disturb his concentration, I waited until we were safely out and pulling onto the street to say, "At the risk of sounding immodest, I learned last summer I have a real knack for this crime-solving thing. And as long as you're a suspect, you can't expect me to stand by and let them arrest you for a crime you didn't commit."

The mood in the truck was heavy, and since Dylan hadn't turned on the radio, we didn't even have music to lighten the tension. I decided it was up to me to take the pressure down a bit with a joke. "I mean where would I find another boyfriend who not only gets along with Fluffy, but defends her to his big brother. You're one in a million, Dylan Carlow."

He snorted, and the pressure lifted. "I really am."

"And humble. I think I forgot to mention it earlier. You're super humble."

He pressed a screen to turn on the radio, and soft music filled the cab of the truck. "But you could write to me in prison. Visit me on Sundays. Maybe even bake me a cake with a file in it."

"An apple cake?" I joked.

"Please, prison would be a respite from apples. A chocolate cake would be nice."

"No apples. Check."

We drove in companionable silence for a few minutes.

"I understand why you want to help find Millikan's killer. And you're right, you do have a knack for mystery solving. It's one of the reasons I can't wait to read your book when you're ready to share it with me. But, please be safe."

"Trust me, I have no desire to tick off another murderer."

The turn signal clicked as he put it on to make the left turn into our driveway. I mean, that's the kind of guy he was. Not another car in sight in either direction, and Dylan used his signal. How could Detective Panchak think for even a millisecond Dylan would kill a man, just because he was a nuisance to him?

The motion-activated flood lights came on, and the driveway was so bright you could've landed a jet on it.

"I guess this means we can't sit in the truck and make out?" Dylan's oh-so-kissable lips turned up at the corners.

"Probably not the best idea. I should get inside soon and make sure things are peaceful between Daddy and Fluffy anyway."

"What's the next move in your investigation?" Dylan twisted in his seat to face me.

"I'd like to learn more about Nesbitt Sharpley-Smythe. I've heard his name, everyone has, but I don't really know anything about him. Plus, as anyone who grew up on *Scooby Doo* could tell you, the real estate developer is always the bad guy."

Dylan threw back his head and laughed. "At the end of

the case, are you going to pull a rubber mask off the apple monster to reveal Sharpley-Smythe?"

"Maybe I will."

His smile faded. "He's a powerful man. And don't let high school memories of Mallory fool you into underestimating her and thinking she isn't too. Even if they aren't the murderers, they are not nice people, and you don't want to be their enemy."

I held up my hands. "Hey, I don't want to be anybody's enemy. I'm just trying to keep my sweetie out of jail."

I struggled against the tide of high school students as I fought my way up the hall of Maple Hills Regional High School to reach the Language Arts department office. No Fluffy with me today, as I had to go right to work after my quick visit to Jeremy, but I did have a huge basket of cinnamon apple muffins clutched to my chest.

Sleep evaded me last night, so I finally gave up around five o'clock and got up to bake muffins with some of the bazillion apples we currently had in our kitchen. I figured teachers always like snacks, right? They'd be grateful for them, whereas if I served them to my parents, they might just chuck them at my head like they were baseballs.

Curious students glanced my way, and the volume level of their excited chatter was at eleven. Were we ever that loud? I guess so. The school seemed just like I remembered and different all at the same time. Nothing had really changed in the interior. The same checkerboard red and white tiled linoleum floors in the hallway with maroon lockers lining the walls. But, I remembered it all as being bigger.

Finally, I reached the office, and rapped on the closed door.

"Come in," Jeremy's voice called out.

"Hello, Mr. Patterson. I came in for extra help," I said in a falsetto voice.

Jeremy looked up from the papers he was grading. His nose was scrunched up as he peered at me. "Amanda! I couldn't imagine who the heck it was with that ridiculous voice."

I hoisted the basket. "Just me. I come bearing baked goods."

He narrowed his eyes. "Apple muffins?"

"Yes. What else? It's apples all day at the Seldon house this month."

"Trouble in apple paradise?" Jeremy grabbed a muffin, pulled off a bit of the crumble topping, and popped it in his mouth. "Oh, this is good."

"Don't sound so surprised. I can bake. It's Dylan's mom's recipe. She emailed it to me. And to answer your question, there is not trouble in apple paradise. Just a whole lot of apples."

"You and Dylan's mom are emailing? Sounds serious."

"She's a nice lady and she has a wealth of apple recipes to share, from her beach house in Myrtle Beach."

An older lady entered the room and sniffed the air. "Do I smell cinnamon?"

I recognized her as my senior year Language Arts teacher. "Hello, Mrs. Bender. It's so good to see you. It's me—"

"Amanda Seldon," she interrupted as she grabbed a muffin from the basket. "I remember you. Always one of my best students. Jeremy tells me you've written an excellent book. I can't wait to read it."

My cheeks grew hot, and I knew my face was roughly

the same color as the lockers in the hallway. "Thank you. I hope you like it."

"I'm sure I will," she said around a mouthful of muffin. "You always had a knack for fiction writing." Her gaze caught on the round clock over the doorway, and she grabbed another muffin and wrapped it in a tissue from the box on Jeremy's desk. "I've got to run to class. Thanks for the treats, Amanda. Teachers always appreciate food."

"You're welcome. Until apple season is over, I'll be bringing in so many baked goods, you'll be sick of seeing me."

Mrs. Bender beamed at me. "I very much doubt it, my dear." She hoisted her muffin into the air and announced like a battle cry, "Once more into the breach!"

She closed the door behind her, and I sat down in the chair across from Jeremy's desk. "She was always my favorite teacher."

"Wait until you get to know her as a grown-up. She's a pistol." He shoveled practically an entire muffin in his mouth.

The rows of maroon yearbooks on the shelves behind Jeremy caught my eye. "Hey, did you know Adrian Van Dyke when he was a student here?"

He swallowed hastily. "I did. Why?"

"I talked to his mother the other day—"

"Is this about Millikan's murder?" He bounced in his seat. "It is, isn't it?"

I nodded my head. "It is. She really hated him, and Mrs. Prattleworth saw her car parked at the condo the day he died. I wanted to try to find out why she was there, so Aunt Lori sent me to town hall to drop off her property tax."

"I can't imagine Bitsy dropping by to visit Millikan.

She hated him with a white hot passion. What did she say she was doing there?"

"She denied she was there."

"Lynn Prattleworth sees all, and she's never wrong. If she says Bitsy was at the condo, then she was. So, why are you interested in Adrian?"

"I'm just curious about him. His accident devastated her, and I'd heard he might not be the innocent she thinks he is. At least as far as his accident is concerned. I thought if he'd been your student, you might have some insight."

Jeremy leaned his chair back and steepled his fingers as he pondered. "He was very quiet in high school. Kept to himself."

"He was shy?" I asked. I could relate, I'd been really shy when I was younger too.

"Not shy, exactly. Just reserved. He wasn't interested in any of the other kids."

"Why do you think he was standoffish?"

He held out his hands, palms up. "I don't know, but I suspect it had to do with his mother. His dad took off when he was little, and Adrian became the sole focus of all of his mother's attention. You talked to her, you saw what she's like."

"She was a little tiring," I said.

"And you only talked to her for a few minutes. Imagine being her whole world, and you can see where Adrian was coming from. I always felt a little sorry for the kid. And she had high expectations for him. When she'd come in for parent-teacher conferences, she always wanted to know what more he could do. More? He was a straight A student in all his classes, not just mine. But she was obsessed with him getting a scholarship, and going to a good school."

"Where did he go to college?" I asked.

Jeremy tapped his finger on the desk. "I don't remember. A lot of students pass through here, and like I said, he was quiet. But from what I remember people saying after his accident, it was one of those small, private colleges. In Pennsylvania, maybe? You know the kind, where the social life revolves around the Greek system."

"Seems like a funny choice for a loner."

"Evidently, he changed at college. He'd pledged a fraternity, and became kind of a partier."

"I saw a lot of people like him at UMass too. Kids with strict parents who went crazy once they were on their own."

He nodded. "I guess it's what happened with him too. He turned twenty-one his junior year. Rumor has it, that summer, he spent more time at Oh Denny Boy's than he did at home."

"You mean the summer of his accident?"

"Yep. Bitsy blamed Dennis Milliken, and while he might've played a role, a large part of the blame falls squarely on Adrian. People were saying it wasn't the first time he'd driven drunk after a night of partying at the microbrewery. But Bitsy is blind to his faults."

"And he's in bad shape since the accident?"

Jeremy heaved a sigh. "Yes. He hit his head and had some sort of traumatic brain injury. And spinal damage as well. I haven't seen him myself, but it's what I've heard."

"You haven't seen him? So he doesn't get out much?"

"Not at all. He apparently needs a lot of care, and doesn't leave the house ever. If Bitsy was bad before the accident, she is completely smothering after it. It's a sad story."

"It is, but an avoidable one," I observed.

"True. It's not like he has a disease. If he didn't drink too much and get behind the wheel, he would be back at school for his senior year right now."

"And Bitsy blames Millikan for all of it."

"Right." Jeremy wagged his finger at me. "And her car was seen at his condominium the day he was killed. Do you think Bitsy is the killer?"

I chuffed out a breath. "I really don't know. But she had motive and opportunity."

"What about means? Do we know what killed him?"

"I heard poison, but I don't know what type."

"Would Danny know?" Jeremy asked.

"I'm not sure. He's recused himself, since Dylan is a suspect and the state police have taken over the case."

"Which is ridiculous."

"One hundred percent ludicrous," I agreed and glanced at the clock. "I didn't realize how long we've been talking. I need to get to work at the orchard."

"If you get any more apple recipes from Mrs. Carlow, the teachers here would all appreciate them. I can stick them in the teachers' lounge, and they might erect a statue to you in front of the school."

I chuckled, as I hoisted my tote bag over my shoulder. "Me holding an apple up to the heavens."

"I'll get the art department on it," Jeremy joked. "So what's next with the case?"

"I guess I need to learn what poison was used, and if Bitsy Van Dyke had access to it."

But how I was going to learn those two things, I had no idea. Detective Panchak was not about to confide in me over lattes and scones at the Sit and Sip. Scones ... hmm... I wonder if the good detective liked apple fritters? And how much tea he would be willing to spill in exchange for some delicious fresh-baked apple goods?

Chapter Eleven

My shift at the orchard was a whirl of tourists, apples, and enough maple candy to send the entire state of Connecticut into sugar shock, so I had no time to ponder how I could find out what poison had killed Dennis Millikan.

I was dressed in my usual work attire, jeans, fleece-lined boots, a thermal Maple Hills Orchard shirt, and a light-weight down vest. I was certain after the apple-palooza events of the day, my hair looked like I'd been dragged through a hedge backwards. So, imagine my glee when I saw a familiar Amazonian blonde towering above most of the people in the barn/shop. Mallory Davisson was here. Huzzah. And looking like she'd just stepped off the runway in Milan.

With her was an elegant gentleman. He was whip thin and almost as tall as Mallory in her mile-high stilettos. His hair was blond or gray, the sort where it was hard to tell which color it was. My guess is his ancestors were among the first to step off the Mayflower. He looked to be that type. Was he the infamous Nesbitt Sharpley-Smythe?

Mallory caught my eye and waved her hand at me. She wanted me to come to her side like a dog? Not fudging likely. I forced a phony smile to my face, pointed to the people paying me for their lifetime supply of candy shaped like maple leaves, and mouthed the word 'sorry'.

Even from this distance, I caught the flash of irritation in her big, blue eyes. She leaned in to speak to the man beside her, in a way which could only be described as intimate. Hmm... could Mallory and Sharpley-Smythe be more than employer and employee? Who was I to judge? I was dating my boss too.

I chuckled to myself and handed the customer her change and bag of candy. "Thank you very much."

The next customer in line approached the cash register, but Mallory shouldered her way past him, and gestured for her companion to come forward. Almost like a courtier, bowing and fluttering her hand while the monarch advances. I experienced a brief pang of sympathy for the woman. It seemed as though she earned every last penny of her hefty paycheck.

"Good day," the man said with a benevolent smile.

"Nesbitt," Mallory interjected before I could say hello and tell them oh-so-politely to get out of the way. There were customers waiting. "This is Amanda Seldon. Amanda, may I present Nesbitt Sharpley-Smythe."

The parents of the family they had cut off in line both gasped at the mention of the multi-billionaire's name. The corners of his mouth twitched, and in spite of his cool exterior, I knew he enjoyed the adulation.

"Hello, Mallory. Nice to meet you, Mr. Sharpley-Smythe. As you can see, we're terribly busy today."

"I'm dreadfully sorry." He drawled in a way that screamed elite boarding schools and Ivy League colleges.

"We're here to see Dylan. Do you have any idea where he might be?" Mallory asked.

Clearly, she wasn't sorry at all, dreadfully or otherwise. Dreadful, yes. Sorry, no.

"Did you check his office?" I asked, while I leaned to my right and waved the family forward.

They hesitated, and I said, "Please come to the counter, it's your turn."

Mallory physically blocked them, like a linebacker. "Of course we checked his office. He wasn't there. Where else might he be?"

"Possibly out in the orchard. This is harvest time. It's the busiest time of the year for him." I kept my gaze trained on the family, and when I waved them forward again, this time the husband tentatively brushed past Mallory.

"I doubt anyone is busier than Nesbitt, yet here we stand surrounded by people who have seemingly never seen an apple before," Mallory snapped.

My professional smile faded, and my lips turned into a tight, straight line as I glared at Mallory. "Did you have an appointment?"

"Well ... no," she admitted with reluctance. Then puffed up again and added, "But it's Nesbitt Sharpley-Smythe. People make time for him, not the other way around."

Sharpley-Smythe placed a pale, long-fingered hand on her arm. The overhead light glinted off his gold signet ring. "Please, Mallory. It's perfectly fine, Ms. Seldon. We understand, it was frightfully cheeky of us to arrive without an appointment. But since we're here already, do you have any way to reach Mr. Carlow?"

"When I've finished with these customers, I can text him."

Mallory chuffed out a breath, but her boss beamed at me and said, "Splendid. Thank you." He turned to Mallory and said sotto voce, but still loudly enough for anyone in the vicinity to hear, "You catch more flies with honey than with vinegar, my dear. When will you learn?"

Her cheeks flamed, and for a moment I thought she was going to tear the man a new one, but she took a deep breath and said, "I'm sorry, Nesbitt."

Dylan's deep voice called from the back of the queue, "Amanda, do you need help with something? What's holding up the line?"

"You have visitors," I raised my voice and jerked my head at Mallory and her companion.

Dylan's eyes widened, and for a brief moment, I feared he was going to bolt, but he squared his shoulders and advanced through the line of increasingly impatient customers.

"Mallory? What are you doing here? I gave you my answer."

"I was hoping to speak to you myself, Mr. Carlow. Perhaps, we can come to an agreement, man-to-man. I'm Nesbitt Sharpley-Smythe." He held out his hand, which Dylan shook.

The corners of Dylan's mouth turned down as they shook hands. "Mr. Sharpley-Smythe, I'm sorry you've wasted a trip to Maple Hills, but my decision is made."

Sharpley-Smythe raised one narrow shoulder in a graceful gesture. "Please don't worry about the trip, I have a home in Litchfield, so it wasn't far. But, since we're here, perhaps we could take a few moments of your time to speak privately."

Dylan hesitated. He was a supremely polite man, and even though I knew him well enough to know he'd like to yank this guy out by the lapel of his bespoke wool suit, he took a deep breath and answered in a resigned manner, "Fine. Let's go to my office to talk. But I have to warn you, I can only give you ten minutes."

"Dylan, this is *Nesbitt Sharpley-Smythe*," Mallory implored.

"I know. He introduced himself."

"People don't dictate the terms of meetings with him, he—"

Again, her boss placed a restraining hand on her arm and interrupted her to finish her sentence, "I will be happy to accept whatever time you have to give me. Please, lead the way to your office, Mr. Carlow."

Dylan followed Sharpley-Smythe through the crowd, which had parted for him as though he were the second coming.

Mallory frowned at me. "You could have used your influence with Dylan to have made this go more smoothly."

"I'm not really concerned about things going smoothly for you." I reached for a bag of apples from the next customer in line. The crowd closed back up as Dylan and Nesbitt passed by, and I jutted my chin in their direction as I rang up the sale. "You'd better hurry."

She put her hands on her hips and drew in a deep breath. I had no doubt I was in for a classic Mallory Davisson smackdown, but Nesbitt somehow managed to be heard above the chatter of the crowd. "Mallory, are you coming?"

She flashed one last irritated glance my way and then raised her voice. "Of course, Nesbitt. On my way." She shoved her way through the crowd to reach her boss's side.

Sympathy filled my heart for Dylan having to take part in a meeting with these two piranhas, but I knew he could hold his own. When my shift was over, I'd hunt him down to lend support and see how it went.

I moved by rote to keep the line moving, and my mind wandered to something Nesbitt Sharpley-Smythe had said. He owned a home in Litchfield, which was not too far from Maple Hills. I wondered how often he'd been to our town, unnoticed while trying to put together the deal to buy the Carlow's land.

A memory popped into my head, of my conversation with Gary Bullaro the night before. If he was to be believed, then Sharpley-Smythe had business in town with Dennis Millikan too. Since Millikan was one of the most confrontational men I'd ever met, I couldn't imagine he hadn't ticked off Sharpley-Smythe at some point in their dealings.

I shook my head briskly. It was ridiculous to think one of the wealthiest investors in the world would have murdered a small-potatoes owner of a microbrewery. Wasn't it?

I SAT ON THE TAILGATE OF DYLAN'S PICKUP TRUCK, LEANED back on my hands, and turned my face upwards to bask in the warmth the late afternoon sun provided. Next to me, Dylan did the same.

"This is something I never got to do during the workday when I was a VP of human resources in Los Angeles." I snuck a peek at him, before turning back to admire the view, and the warmth came from within my heart as well as the sunshine. "Thanks."

He glanced at me and his lips turned up in a quizzical manner. "For what? Letting you work at my orchard and deal with a steady influx of not-always-polite leaf peepers? You're welcome."

"I actually really appreciate the job, but I just meant thank you for sharing this experience with me." Sitting up straight I waved my arm in an arc at the rows of apple trees, laden with red fruit, the hills beyond them, and the leaves glowing crimson and gold in the setting sun. "Wow. Just wow. I grew up seeing this every day, but didn't really understand how fortunate I was to see it. Cities have their appeal too. I was happy in LA, but this is awe-inspiring."

Dylan squinted into the light and bobbed his head. "You're right. At this time of year, I tend to look out over the orchard and only see the work that needs to be done, but it is pretty amazing."

"Speaking of coming back to Maple Hills, how did your meeting with Mallory and her boss go?"

He heaved a sigh. "It was a pain. They refuse to accept the fact I don't want to sell my land."

"Were they really pushy about it?"

"Sharpley-Smythe is too smooth to be overtly pushy, but he was relentless. And then I caught a little byplay between them, and Mallory started coming on to me."

"You mean coming on strong with her sales pitch?" I asked, fairly certain it was not, in fact, what Dylan meant.

"Nope. Flirting. Totally inappropriate in any business meeting, but especially weird in this one."

"Why?"

"Because before she started with the come-on, I was picking up on a vibe between them. Like their relationship might be more than business. You know what I mean?"

I swatted his bicep and exclaimed, "I do! I thought the same thing when they were in the store earlier."

"It wasn't anything specific, just a feeling I had," Dylan said.

"And you're right, it does make it more unseemly if he was encouraging his own girlfriend to flirt with you to seal the deal. What did he say to make you think that was what was happening?"

"He didn't say anything. He just looked pointedly between us and when he caught Mallory's eye, he jerked his head in my direction." Dylan paused and then shook his head. "Not really a jerk, it was almost imperceptible, but I definitely picked up on it. And apparently, so did Mallory, because right afterwards, she went into vixen mode."

"Yuck."

"My thoughts exactly. Obviously, it didn't work."

"Trust me, I never thought for a moment it would. So, how did you leave things? Are they slinking back to New York with their tails between their legs?"

"Unfortunately, they are not. Mallory produced another offer from her briefcase and left it with me to review, and said she'd be in touch."

"Joy." I rolled my eyes.

"Hopefully, it will be the last offer, and they'll start considering another location for their development."

We sat in silence for a moment, enjoying the view as the hills and orchard glowed in the golden light of the setting sun. I sat up with a jolt. "What time is it?"

"You got a bus to catch?" One corner of Dylan's mouth quirked up.

"No, but I do need to get moving. I'm going out with Cara and Jeremy tonight, and I need to get home, feed Fluffy, and then try to make myself presentable."

"The Three Musketeers on the town, huh? Where are you guys headed?"

"I wanted to go to Oh Denny Boy's just to see what it was like. Morbid curiosity, I know, but with everything going on, I wanted to check it out and see if it was as bad as everyone says it is."

"Trust me, it is. But it's closed. Dennis Millikan was the owner and the manager, so without him, they're kind of lost at sea there. I guess it will be closed until we find out who it belongs to now."

"I still would've liked to have seen it, but Cara vetoed me, so we're going for drinks and appetizers at the Maple Hills Arms. Mitch is watching the kids tonight, so she wanted to get dressed up and go somewhere nice."

He whistled low between his teeth. "Fancy."

"Want to come?"

"No thanks, even if I wasn't completely beat, I wouldn't want to intrude on Three Musketeers time. I know how important it is to you."

I bumped my shoulder against his. "You're pretty wonderful."

"Yes, yes I am." He winked at me, before hopping off the bed of his truck and holding out his hands to help me down.

Once I was on the ground he pulled me in for a hug. I rested my head against his shoulder; I was average height, but Dylan was so tall it put me in perfect position to do so. "I wish I could stay with you a little longer, but Fluffy waits for no woman. And I don't dare leave her alone with my mom for too long. I love my folks, but I can't wait for the deal on my condo to close, so Fluff and I have our own space again."

He pressed a kiss to the top of my head. "It will be nice for lots of reasons."

My pulse raced, and I mentally willed the real estate agent to pick up the pace with the closing. "Yes, it will."

Chapter Twelve

"It was nice of Eric to be our chauffeur tonight." I shrugged off my black, cashmere pashmina and settled into my seat at the posh cocktail bar in the Maple Hills Arms.

Jeremy took the seat across from me at our round table. "Ride shares aren't exactly a thing in a town with a population of three-thousand, so it's a safer option for Cara's big night out on the town."

"You better believe it. I'm so excited for a night out without the kids. It was fun getting all dressed up, but Eric could've joined us," Cara sat in the seat next to me.

My friend did look drop-dead gorgeous in her black cigarette pants and black silk top. A diamond necklace sparkled in the dim lighting of the bar, and the only pop of color were her red stilettos. Which brought my petite friend to roughly the same height as me. With her dark hair cut in a stylish short, pixie style, she had a sort of Audrey Hepburn vibe going.

"He didn't want to intrude on Three Musketeers time,"

Jeremy said and picked up the large, leatherbound cocktail menu and wine list.

A waitress dressed in black pants, a white shirt, and black bow tie came over to take our order.

"We'll start with drinks, and get some appetizers in a bit," said Cara as she perused the menu. "And I think I'll have the Bootlegger's martini. With extra olives, please."

"I'd like the Maple Hills old fashioned, please." Jeremy handed the menu to me.

"A Manhattan for me," I said without even looking at the menu.

The waitress jotted down our orders and headed for the bar.

"You didn't even look at their specialty cocktails." Cara pouted.

"I love a Manhattan on a chilly night, and those were in short supply when I lived in LA. I was looking forward to this Manhattan all day." My phone buzzed in the small clutch I'd carried, much smaller than my usual handbag, but since I'd gotten dressed up in my Black-Watch plaid mini, fuzzy black sweater, tights, and booties, the small black baguette was a better choice than my giant, brown tote bag.

"Your silly little purse is ringing," Jeremy said with a cheeky grin.

I pulled out my phone, and my heart raced. "It's my real estate agent. Maybe she has news. Hello, this is Amanda." Between the jazz music on the sound system and chattering other patrons, I struggled to hear. I stuck a finger in my other ear, but it didn't block the sound. I raised my voice. "I'm sorry, I'm at out at a bar and I can't hear you. Let me run outside where it's quieter, and I'll call you right back."

As I disconnected the call and stood up, Jeremy teased

me with a twinkle in his eyes, "I don't think you actually needed to raise your voice. Your agent isn't the one in a noisy bar."

Wrapping myself in the pashmina, I rolled my eyes. "Hardy har har. But I have to admit you have a valid point. I'm just so nervous. I really, really want this condo."

Cara waved her hands toward the door. "Go. Call her."

I bustled through the lobby, and the bellman rushed to pull the door open before I charged through it. "Sorry," I called over my shoulder and hurried outside. A family had just pulled up, and their kids spilled out of the minivan chattering excitedly while the parents unloaded the luggage and called for the bellman. Huh. Not much quieter out here. There was a small alleyway between the hotel and the building next to it, and I scooted into it to make my call.

The alley was pitch black and nowhere I would've ever ventured into in Los Angeles or New York, but I figured it would be safe as houses in Maple Hills. I shivered and pulled my black pashmina closer around me. Between the unlit alley and my dark outfit I was probably invisible to any passersby.

Before I could call my real estate agent back, a familiar voice sounded from the end of the alley. Mallory Davisson, oh joy.

I took a step farther back into the alley, in the hopes she wouldn't see me. Tonight was all about Three Musketeers fun, and I didn't want her harshing my happiness.

"The man is dead, Nesbitt."

A low chuckle greeted her words, not the response I expected.

"And may his black soul be tormented for eternity," drawled Nesbitt Sharpley-Smythe.

"He was murdered," Mallory hissed the last word. "You might want to ease up on that sort of talk."

I decided my call could wait for a couple of minutes, because their conversation about murder made my sleuthing radar ping.

"Do you want me to pretend to be sorry Millikan is dead? I cannot. The man was a fool, and we never should've entered into our arrangement with him. His pathetic attempts to discredit Carlow, and ruin his new cider product line did nothing to harm the man."

I smothered a gasp. They were behind Millikan's belligerent attitude toward Dylan? Why would a multi-billionaire care about a small cider operation in the middle of nowhere?

"I did tell you Dylan is the golden child of Maple Hills, and nothing a newcomer to town had to say would carry any weight with the locals, but you wouldn't listen."

I could practically see Mallory's full-lips pouting, based on her sullen tone of voice.

Nesbitt tsked his tongue. "Saying 'I told you so' is most unbecoming, my dear. However, you are an expert on this backwater, and I should've paid you more heed. In a less provincial town, Oh Denny Boy's would've been a smashing success and put Carlow's fledgling hard cider operation down in no time. And then the man would've been in dire financial straits and willing to sell his land."

So that was their game. Little did they know, it was doomed to fail from the start, because Dylan was not in dire financial straits, he was just trying to expand his business. And a man like Sharpley-Smythe would never understand the Carlow family's emotional connection to their land.

While lost in thought, I'd missed what Mallory replied, but heard Nesbitt's next words loud and clear.

"And not only did the man fail in our simple task, but then he turned on me like a cornered weasel and tried to blackmail me. Me, Nesbitt Sharpley-Smythe. Who did he think he was?"

"A smarter man would've known better than to extort you, darling, but Millikan was most decidedly not a smarter man." Mallory laughed softly, and her high heels clicked on the sidewalk as they strolled away from the entrance to the alley.

While I couldn't honestly say I was sorry Millikan was dead, I was not inclined to laugh about it either. But then, he hadn't been blackmailing me. And blackmail was one of your classic motives for murder.

My hand shook as I tapped the screen of my phone to place my call, and this time it wasn't with excitement about my impending new condo.

Was I honestly thinking one of the wealthiest men in the world might have murdered Dennis Millikan? Yes, yes I was.

As I sank into my seat in the bar, I slipped my pashmina off my shoulders and onto the back of the chair while I took a hurried sip of my cocktail to soothe my nerves.

"Well, tell us! Did you get the condo?" Cara bounced in her seat. I gulped some more of my Manhattan, and the bourbon burned as it went down.

"Easy there. Something's wrong, I can tell. What the heck happened outside?" Jeremy furrowed his brow and peered at me over the small lamp in the center of our table.

"You won't believe it." I leaned over the table and whispered.

"Forget believe it, I won't *hear* it, if you don't speak a little louder." Cara laughed and took a sip of her almost empty drink. I guess I'd been outside longer than I'd realized.

I'd shifted in my seat in my attempt to lean in and be heard without talking too loudly, "I went outside to make my call, and I overheard something very interesting—"

"Please do share," Nesbitt Sharpley-Smythe's voice sounded behind me and I jumped a foot off my seat and clutched my hand to my pounding heart.

I jerked my head around and saw Mallory in a slinky, red silk dress, and Nesbitt in yet another bespoke suit, which probably cost more than my condo. "Oh, hello. I didn't see you there." My voice trembled. I needed to get it together. I didn't want these two vipers to know what I'd heard. "What are you doing here tonight?'

"We're staying at the hotel. We just stopped in for a nightcap," Nesbitt replied. "But we interrupted your conversation. Please continue."

Man, the guy really wanted to know what I'd over-heard. I reached for my drink and realized I didn't need to get sloshed. My wits had to be sharp against these two. But my throat was parched, so instead, I grabbed my water glass and took a deep sip from it.

"I'd assumed you were staying with your parents, Mallory, but I'd forgotten they'd moved to southern Connecticut. Greenwich, was it?" Jeremy asked.

"Mm-hmm. They wanted to be closer to me in Manhattan," Mallory replied to Jeremy, but kept her gaze firmly trained on me. "Thank heavens this hotel opened, otherwise I'd be staying at the Dew Drop Inn. Which you know all too well is a dump, from your days as a maid there, Amanda."

My molars ground together. I was not about to put up with this snob dissing the Dew Drop. It might not be fancy, but Carol ran a tight ship, and it was always clean and well-maintained. "The Dew Drop is not a dump, Mallory. And yes, working there was my first job, and I'm proud of it." I tapped my finger to my chin. "Now where was your first job again?"

"She swept up the hair at Shear Madness," Cara piped up in an overly helpful tone.

"Right, she used to clean up other people's dirty hair. Now, how is that any better than being a chambermaid?" I asked.

"They'd be about equal in the lousy first job contest, I'd say," Jeremy said.

Nesbitt glared at Mallory. "You interrupted your old schoolmate, and she was just about to share some news she overheard when we arrived at the table."

Chastened, Mallory's shoulders drooped and her gaze dropped to the floor. "I'm sorry, Nesbitt."

I looked between them with open curiosity. What was the deal between this odd couple? I decided to fudge the truth a bit, and tell him only part of what I'd been about to share with my friends. "It's nothing you would've been interested in, my real estate agent just called, and the offer on the condominium has been accepted. I'm officially a homeowner again."

Cara squealed and jumped up and clasped me in a hug. "I'm so happy for you!"

"Great news!" Jeremy exclaimed.

Nesbitt narrowed his eyes, and his searching gaze penetrated my soul. I attempted to keep my expression neutral, because he obviously suspected I'd overheard his incriminating blackmail confession. "Thanks, guys. I'm really happy about it."

"Congratulations," Nesbitt said, but cocked his head. "I'm not altogether sure it's what you were about to say when we interrupted, but it is very good news indeed. Perhaps, we can talk more when next we meet."

Or perhaps I could have a root canal with no anesthesia, because it sounded like about as much fun as telling one of the most powerful men in the world I knew he'd been blackmailed by a man who ended up murdered.

"YOU LOOK LIKE SOMETHING THE BEAST ATTACKED IN A frenzy. Then dragged through a hedge," Aunt Lori said as I entered the library the next morning.

I pushed my sunglasses up on my nose, not ready to take them off, even though I was inside. "Three Musketeers night out last night."

"Say no more." She held up her hands.

I clutched Fluffy in one arm, and the bag I held in the other crinkled as I waved it at her. "I brought celebratory bagels."

She narrowed her eyes at me. "I think you've done enough celebrating for a while, Mandy-bel. Besides, what are we celebrating?" She flashed me a roguish grin and reached for the bag, "But I'll never turn down a free bagel."

"I got the condo! I found out last night."

"Wonderful news! I'm thrilled for you!" She hip checked the swinging door to come out from behind the circulation desk and pulled me in for a breathtaking hug, while she still clutched the bag of bagels. The garlic aroma from the everything bagel usually was delightful, but this morning, my stomach churned, and I pulled away slightly.

"I'm sorry I missed last night, based on how you're feeling this morning. Where did you go? I was at Hitchcock's and didn't see you there."

"We went to the cocktail lounge at the Maple Hills Arms. It was really nice."

"It's a great spot. A real added attraction for the town." She went back behind the circulation desk and gestured for me to follow. "Put The Beast down and follow me. We can sit back here and have our bagels."

I left Fluffy on her leash, but set her on the floor. We followed Aunt Lori into her office. I didn't even have it in me to tell her to stop calling Fluffy by the insulting nickname. With a sigh, I flopped into a chair at a worktable behind the counter.

"Are you going to take your sunglasses off? Since we're, y'know ... indoors."

"The lighting in here is very bright, so I think I'll just leave them on for now."

"Do you want coffee? We have a little coffee bar in the library now. I can get us each a cup."

"I would pay whatever price you ask for a cup of strong coffee."

She threw back her head and laughed, and the sound went through my head like a knife. "You poor thing. Auntie Lori is on the job."

"I can always count on you. Particularly in a hangover situation."

As she walked over to the coffee bar along the wall near the main entrance, she called over her shoulder. "And you don't even have to pay me a thing. Just promise to find Millikan's real killer so the police get off Hitch's back."

"I still can't believe they think he killed Millikan. It's almost as ridiculous as suspecting Dylan of doing it."

Lori came back with two mugs and placed one in front of me. I picked it up and inhaled deeply before taking a sip. Ahh ... that's the ticket. I might even be up to eating the sesame bagel I bought for myself after all. I'd been thinking I'd have to save it for lunch. But a little carb-y goodness and caffeine might just get me through this day.

"Maybe even more ridiculous, because Hitch is the most laid-back man on the planet. Seriously, I can't imagine him bestirring himself to poison Millikan. Especially just for being a jerk to him. He's run the tavern for years, and it's made him a pro at handling obnoxious jerks."

I smeared cream cheese on my bagel. "You have a point there."

"Detective Panchak contacted him late yesterday afternoon, and he wants Hitch to come in this morning to talk." She put air quotes around the last word, and then went back to prepping her bagel. "Talk? Interrogate is more like it."

"And there are so many other suspects." I took a bite of my bagel, and there might've been moaning. I'm not proud, but it was that good.

"And much more likely suspects." She waved her bagel at me.

Fluffy stood between us, staring fixedly back and forth between our bagels, as if she were at a tennis match.

"I know, right?" I mumbled around a mouthful of bagel, before I swallowed hastily. "I mean just last night I overheard Mallory Davisson and Nesbitt Sharpley-Smythe talking, and they have one big old motive."

Lori's eyes opened wide over her coffee cup as she sipped. "Really? What?"

"Blackmail."

She gasped. "Millikan was blackmailing them? About what?"

"I don't know all the details yet, but believe me, I'll be looking into it. Unlike the police detective so set on Hitch and Dylan that he's ignoring all the valid suspects."

"And what about the other guy? The out-of-towner who Millikan did dirty in the business deal?"

"Gary Bullaro. Yes, he's another prime suspect."

"And don't forget what Lynn Prattleworth told us when we were at your condo. She saw Bitsy Van Dyke's car there the day he died. What was she doing there?"

"Nothing good."

"Although I can't really see mousy little Bitsy murdering someone."

I shrugged. "You never know what people are capable of doing. I mean, I agree, it's hard to imagine, but she did detest Millikan. And she acted darned suspicious when I talked to her at Town Hall. She might've snapped."

"I guess. So what's your next move?"

While I chewed on a delectable bite of bagel, I mulled over her question. After I swallowed, I said, "I guess try to find out more about the blackmail. Although, I'm a little nervous about approaching Sharpley-Smythe, and Mallory won't tell me anything."

"Why nervous? Is it because he's so rich and powerful?"

"And possibly a murderer," I added. "Plus, I think he overheard me telling Cara and Jeremy I overheard him last night."

"That's a lot of overhearing." Aunt Lori chuckled. "As an author you might want to watch repeating words in the same sentence."

"Please, I'm lucky I'm able to form any sentences this morning."

Lori tapped her fingernails on the table. "Hmm... I can see where a rich, powerful, potential killer being aware you know he was being blackmailed by someone who turned up murdered would be a situation you'd want to avoid."

A cheery tune played from my purse where I'd slung it on the floor when I sat down. I held up my index finger. "Hold that thought. It's Dylan's ring tone." I pulled out my phone and read his text. The bagel sat in my stomach like lead when I read his message. "Oh for the love of apples."

"Orchard problems?" Lori arched one perfectly shaped eyebrow.

"No, murder suspect problems. Detective Panchak has called Dylan in to talk also. This afternoon."

"Hitch is this morning, so he must be after him. Do you think it means they suspect Hitch more?" White showed all around the center of Lori's green eyes.

"Or they just need to clear up a point with Hitch, and are planning to arrest Dylan afterwards."

Lori pressed her hands onto her cheeks, which had paled at my words. "Oh, no."

I crumpled my little paper napkin and tossed it on the table. "It sounds like I need to get over my nerves and see what I can find out from Sharpley-Smythe. Pronto."

Chapter Thirteen

Caffeine and carbs worked their magic yet again, and I'd managed to work through another chapter of Jeremy's edits on my manuscript. I glanced at the large clock over the fireplace in the library and sighed. Time had gotten away from me, and now I couldn't find Sharpley-Smythe and wheedle more information about the blackmail before my shift at the orchard.

Fluffy's tags jingled as she woke up and shook under the table. Aunt Lori had kindly allowed me to let her stay with me, so long as no other patrons came into the library. There was some insulting talk about liability and dog bite lawsuits, but I chose to ignore them, since it meant I didn't have to make an extra trip to drop her at my parents' house.

A young man emerged from the back reading room and glanced at the circulation desk. If I wasn't mistaken, relief flickered across his face to find it unoccupied. Aunt Lori had stepped away to unpack an order of books in the workroom, but why would he be relieved she wasn't there? He was too young for her, but Aunt Lori's charms generally crossed all age barriers, and people young and old were drawn to her many charms.

Fluffy stepped out from under the table and barked. The low, deep sound she made when she wanted to intimidate someone, in the hopes they would think she was not basically a stuffed animal come to life. The man jumped and twisted his head to look in our direction. His eyes were wide, and his jaw hung to the floor.

"Sorry." I picked up Fluffy, who took advantage of the higher elevation to glare and growl. "I thought we were alone in the building. She won't hurt you." I mentally crossed my fingers.

He nodded curtly, and made for the front door. I noticed for the first time he held a cane in his hand, and leaned on it heavily as he limped away from Fluffy and me. The door slammed shut behind him, and I put Fluffy back on the ground to pack up my notes and laptop.

"Did I hear The Beast barking?" Aunt Lori emerged from the stairwell.

"You did, but it's under control. Some guy was in the reading room, and he startled us when he came out. I thought we were the only ones here."

Lori pursed her glossy, peach lips. "I didn't see anyone come in, did you?"

"Not while I've been here. Fluffy would definitely have let us know if someone had come into the library."

"I did run to the ladies room a few minutes before you got here, so maybe he came in then. Did he need help with anything?"

"Nope. He just hustled out the front door after he saw Fluffy and me. Well, hustled is an exaggeration. He had quite a limp, and walked with a cane. But he didn't seem inclined to stick around after he spotted us."

"Young man? With sort of wavy brown hair?"

"Yes. He was about your height, and slightly built. I didn't recognize him, but I'd guess he was only a kid when I left town fifteen years ago." The notion a grown man had been a child when I left town hit me in the chest like a wrecking ball. "And when did I get to be one hundred and ten years old?"

Lori chuckled. "Now you know what it was like for me watching you grow up." Her smiled faded. "I think I know who he was."

"And why does it look like it's flipping you out?"

"Because it is a little bit. I think it was Adrian Van Dyke. I hope he didn't hear us talking about our suspicions of his mother. In case she's innocent, I'd hate for her to know what we were thinking of her."

"And if she's guilty, I'd hate it even more. Trust me, having a killer know you suspect them does not lead to anything good."

I pondered the implications of Adrian Van Dyke telling his mother we suspected her of murder as I walked out of the library. With a deep exhalation, I placed Fluffy on the sidewalk. No use worrying about it now, the proverbial horse was out of the barn.

Lost in my thoughts, I started at the angry voice in front of the Maple Hills Arms, and couldn't believe my eyes. Gary Bullaro poked his index finger at Nesbitt Sharpley-Smythe while he read the gazillionaire the riot act.

As I took a few tentative steps closer, the better to hear them, I pretended to search through my bag. Hey, I couldn't just stand there and gape at them while I eavesdropped. Subtlety, thy name is Amanda.

"But Oh Denny Boy's was all me. I was the brains

behind the whole business. All Dennis had was the name," Bullaro roared.

Sharpley-Smythe dusted a piece of invisible lint off of his immaculate suit jacket. "But the name is all I needed, my good man. Business acumen, I already have in spades."

Gary Bullaro deflated like an underfilled balloon. "But you need a manager, and I could run Oh Denny Boy's for you."

"I have plenty of people on my payroll who could do the job, if I decide to leave the microbrewery open."

"But it might not be your decision to make. We don't know what's in Dennis's will. Maybe he left his share of the business to me."

A slow, sly smile oozed across Sharpley-Smythe's face. "Do you honestly think I got to where I am today by crafting shoddy business contracts? No, I'm afraid upon his death his interest in the business reverts to me."

"What?" The other man staggered back a step, and all the color drained out of his face.

"Oh my, it seems you had expectations following Millikan's death. I hope you weren't willing to kill for them, because you're doomed to disappointment. Now, if you'll excuse me, I see someone with whom I need to speak."

My only excuse for standing still as a statue and not realizing Sharpley-Smythe referred to me was because I was laser focused on what he'd just said. Had Bullaro really expected to inherit Dennis Millikan's share of the business, and if so would he murder his old friend for it? People had killed for less.

"Ms. Seldon, what a delightful piece of serendipity to find you and your... " he sneered and paused long enough to make it insulting. "... charming dog here right now."

I glanced over his shoulder and saw Bullaro turn on his heel and scurry across the street. Serendipity works two ways, and after my initial panic at being confronted by Sharpley-Smythe, I had just been thinking I needed to talk to him, and here he was.

"Hello, Mr. Sharpley-Smythe. I'm surprised to see you in town today."

"Really, why?"

"You mentioned having a home in Litchfield. I'd assumed you'd returned there while Dylan reviews your latest offer."

"I stayed at the Maple Hills Arms last night. Mallory and I had important business to discuss. We were up very late... " his voice trailed off, and he shot the cuff of his shirt under his jacket.

"Discussing?" I suggested. *Is that what the billionaires are calling it these days?*

"Precisely. So much discussing." He beamed at me.

I suppressed a shudder at the mental image. "I'm sorry about your altercation with Mr. Bullaro. It looked upsetting."

"For him perhaps."

"I've spoken to Mr. Bullaro before, and he said Dennis Millikan cheated him out of Oh Denny Boy's. Perhaps he deserves a share of the business."

Sharpley-Smythe wagged his finger. "He most certainly does not. Any person who allowed a buffoon like Dennis Millikan to best them in a business deal has no place in my organization."

"You have a point." Savvy and intelligent were not the adjectives I'd choose to describe Millikan.

He tapped a long, slender finger on his chin as he studied me like he would a sub-par contract, right before tearing it apart. "Word around town is you fancy yourself an amateur sleuth. If you're investigating Millikan's death, you might want to take a closer look at Mr. Bullaro's whereabouts. He certainly had a motive to do away with the man, if only in his mind."

"I wouldn't say I'm a sleuth." Although I totally would. Heck, Fluffy and I took down a killer last summer, but no need to put myself in this man's crosshairs. Sharpley-Smythe as my enemy was not something I needed.

"You mustn't be modest. Your exploits are the talk of the town. And one would hate for you to miss the real murderer by following a false lead."

"A false lead? What do you mean?" I wrinkled my nose.

"I believe you overheard a conversation last night which might paint me in a bad light. About blackmail?"

My heart raced, but I strove to maintain a cool exterior. Here was the very thing I wanted to discuss with him, but I was thrown off my game when he was the one to introduce the topic. "I did hear a snippet of a conversation, but things can be so easily taken out of context and misconstrued. Perhaps you can illuminate me?" Heavens, the man's formal way of speaking must be contagious.

"Mr. Millikan was under the impression he had me at a disadvantage, and he sought to profit from it."

"So he *was* blackmailing you?" My nerves must be transmitting to Fluffy, because she took a step toward Sharpley-Smythe and bared her sharp teeth.

He took a step backward and kept a wary eye on my dog. "She is a fierce, little thing, isn't she?"

"She's very protective of me." I let the meaning hang there between us, in the hope a healthy fear of the Fluffster would prevent him from coming after me, if he was the killer. "I notice you didn't answer my question."

Sharpley-Smythe raised his gaze from Fluffy to my face and smirked. "He was attempting to blackmail me, but he wouldn't have succeeded. Mr. Millikan seemed to think he had leverage over me, regarding my development plans here in town, as well as my relationship with Mallory. Neither are worth a penny to me."

In spite of the disinterest in his voice, he seemed bound and determined to convince me of his lack of motive. "Perhaps he knew something else that would be valuable for you to suppress?"

"I understand you're desperate to find a viable suspect to divert the attention of the police away from your beau, but I'm sorry. I'm not the person you seek. And to be honest, it might work to my advantage to have Mr. Carlow arrested for the murder. He's the only one standing between me and my development plans for Maple Hills."

I gasped, and Fluffy emitted a flurry of high-pitched yips, a sure indicator she was anxious. *Join the club, my girl, so am I.* Because if one of the wealthiest people on the planet found it beneficial for Dylan to be convicted of a crime, then I'm afraid it would be a freight train I couldn't to stop.

His mouth twisted into a self-satisfied smile. "Good day, Ms. Seldon." Without waiting for my reply, he turned and strolled off up Main Street, looking like a man without a worry in the world.

Funny, because the weight of my worries landed on my shoulders like a sky-diving elephant. Now I needed to protect Dylan not only from Detective Panchak, but also from Nesbitt Sharpley-Smythe.

My legs ached after another long afternoon shift at the orchard. I seriously hadn't gotten to sit down for a second, but Fluffy needed to do her business. So here I was, standing around in the dark, while Fluffy examined every tree and fallen leaf on my parents' front yard. The outdoor lights were on, so there was some illumination, but she'd gravitated toward the darkest part of the lawn and for some reason I was edgy and anxious. However, Fluffy was not a dog to be rushed. I tried to walk closer to the house, in hopes of giving her the hint to keep moving, but she just dug her short, little legs in and refused to budge from the maple tree she'd been sniffing.

I heaved a sigh and stretched my back while I waited for her to finish her inspection of the tree bark. My mind wandered to Millikan's death, as it did every time I had a free minute lately. Dylan had come back from the police station shortly before my shift ended, but he had a ton of work to catch up on and told me he'd tell me about it later.

There were dark circles under his eyes, but it could just be a normal autumn condition for an apple orchard owner in New England, and not the fact he'd apparently been grilled by Panchak all afternoon. At least he hadn't been detained.

The suspects ran through my mind. Obviously, Dylan could be discounted. And probably Hitch too. I didn't know the man very well, but Aunt Lori did, and she believed him to be innocent. At least of the murder. No man able to hold Lori's interest could be completely innocent. In spite of my current mood, thinking about my fun-loving aunt brought a smile to my lips.

Hallelujah, Fluffy moved away from the maple tree. I heaved a sigh. Only to move to an oak. Still dressed in my work clothes, I shivered in the cool, night air and wished I'd put on a warmer coat. I tentatively tried to encourage Fluffy to move it along, only to have her chuff out a breath and glare at me, while digging in her little, doggie heels.

Okay, back to thinking over the suspects. The most likely were Gary Bullaro, Nesbitt Sharpley-Smythe, Bitsy Van Dyke, and Mallory Davisson. I chuckled and admitted to myself the last name on my list might be personal. But, Mallory had never been a nice person, and her meteoric rise in the business world probably hadn't made her any nicer. They all had motive to eliminate Dennis Millikan, but to be fair, so had everyone who'd ever met the man.

Fluffy lifted her head, her ears pricked, and her body tensed. I licked my lips and glanced around nervously. What did she hear? There was a copse of trees between my parents' house and the street, and I heard something rustling there.

Most likely it was just a deer, but Fluffy had found a new hobby in Connecticut, chasing deer. One day when Fluffy wasn't on the leash she took off after a doe, and I had to run like an Olympic track star to catch her. In an effort for full disclosure, I will admit I am not an Olympic-caliber runner, and I was sucking serious wind by the time I caught her. I didn't want a repeat performance on a cold, dark night.

The rustling stopped, and I eased my death grip on the leash. Perhaps the animal had gone the other way, away from where we stood. Fluffy cocked her head, but maintained her defensive stance by the oak tree. Did she still hear or see something, with her superior canine senses? Or was she just ready for a little action and not willing to abandon the hope of a deer to chase?

Another crinkle of fallen leaves from the wooded area made me clutch the leash again. Guess my girl did hear something I didn't. I peered into the trees, but the area in between our exterior lights and the Rosenberg's house was pitch black.

"C'mon, Fluff. Let's go inside." I shivered, and this time it wasn't from the cold. What if it wasn't a deer? Not to be dramatic or anything, but there was a killer out there, and I was investigating the case.

Without warning, Fluffy lurched forward, barking furiously. The woven leash dug into my hands where I grasped it as tightly as I could, in an attempt to hold back my very determined shih tzu.

Fluffy's barking was drowned out by a loud bang. Was some yahoo out here setting off fireworks? I look to the sky, and only saw a blanket of twinkling stars on this cold, clear night. Another explosive sound made me jump, and this time I saw a flash of light from the woods.

It wasn't fireworks. Someone was shooting at us.

Chapter Fourteen

Wood exploded from the tree right behind Fluffy as the projectile hit its mark. Acting purely on instinct, I dove for my furry friend and clasped her in my arms, as I tried to keep us as small and low to the ground as possible.

Another blast and more wood splinters showered down on us. Fluffy shivered in my arms, but it was hard to tell because I was shaking so hard. We needed to get out of here. Now. But I had no idea how to without standing up and getting shot in the process. My phone was in my pocket, and I tried to shift Fluffy where I clutched her beneath me to free one arm to reach for it, and another shot rang out while I did so.

"Stop shooting right now! I've called the police." My father's voice boomed from the front step. "Leave my daughter alone, you—" The air turned blue with the string of words at the end of the sentence. Yep, Dad was good and furious.

The welcome sound of a siren in the distance met my ears. It was too soon to breathe a sigh of relief, but my

shaking subsided a bit. Not Fluffy's though, as she didn't
know what the sirens meant. She struggled against my tight
hold and whimpered. Even though she still trembled, my
girl was ready to go after whoever was out to harm us. I
couldn't bring myself to think the word 'kill', so I just went
with 'harm'.

"Are you all right, Amanda?" My father's voice shook.

"I am. We both are," I called out with a quavery voice,
which probably did nothing to allay my father's fears.

Leaves and brush rustled as someone crashed through
the woods. Fortunately for me, they seemed to be running
towards the street. A car engine roared to life.

From my vantage point on the ground, I saw the
Rosenberg's yard suddenly flooded with light, and Cara's
dad ran toward the street. Dressed in flannel pants and a
plaid robe, the burly man looked like a bear woken from
his hibernation. He seemed about as angry as one would
be too.

Footsteps ran toward us. My mother cried out, "If
you're all right, why aren't you moving? Amanda?"

"I'm okay, Mommy." But, oh yeah, the psycho with the
gun had pulled away, so I could move again. I think I'd
been literally frozen with fear. I sat up, but clutched Fluffy
tightly to my chest. She pressed her velvety cheek against
mine. We sat like that, still trembling, until my parents
reached us.

Both of them dropped to their knees and clasped Fluffy
and me in one big, Seldon family hug.

Mr. Rosenberg appeared in our driveway from the
street. He bent over and panted out between breaths, "He
got away."

Mrs. Rosenberg lightly ran across their yard to ours.
Cara took after her mom, and Mrs. R. was petite and in
better shape for sprinting around in the night than her

husband was. "What were you thinking running after a person with a gun?" Her angry words were softened by the tremble in her voice as she wrapped her arms around her husband.

He straightened up and embraced her right back. "I wanted to see if I could get a license plate number."

"Could you?" My dad's voice was muffled, since we were still sitting on the lawn holding each other as if we'd never let go. Even Fluffy, who generally only tolerated so much human affection, snuggled contentedly in the center of the Seldon sandwich.

The wail of the sirens grew louder, and I could see the red and blue lights flashing through the trees.

"Sorry, I couldn't." Mr. Rosenberg had caught his breath. "He didn't put his headlights on, and it was too dark. By the time I reached the street, he was too far away. I gotta start going to the gym with you, Michael. I'm out of shape."

The police car squealed to a stop in our driveway, followed closely by a dark SUV. An officer got out of their car, and Danny Carlow jumped out of the SUV and made a beeline toward our little group.

"Amanda? Are you all right? What in the Sam Hill happened here?" He roared.

"I'm okay, Danny."

"Good, because I didn't want to have to tell my brother you'd been shot." He tried to grin in an attempt to lighten the mood, but it was more of a grimace.

"Someone shot at me, or maybe at Fluffy, it seemed like they were aiming lower than if I was the target. You can see where the bullets hit the tree."

His eyebrows met in the middle as he studied the oak tree. "You guys need to get in the house, so we can tape off this area."

Right. My parents front yard was a crime scene now, because someone wanted to harm me or Fluffy. "You're probably counting the days until I close on my condo right about now."

WE SAT AROUND THE KITCHEN TABLE, WHERE MY MOM HAD made hot cocoa for us. Complete with mini marshmallows on top, just like she used to do when I'd come in from ice skating on the pond when I was a kid. I cupped my hands around the mug, welcoming the warmth. Even though we were cozy in the house now, I still shivered a bit. I may have been in shock.

Danny had come inside with us, but left his officers outside to begin the investigation. "So you couldn't see anything, Mr. Rosenberg?"

"No, I'm sorry, he was too fast for me."

"He? So it was a man?" Danny latched onto the pronoun and barked out his question. Even in plain clothes, he was still clearly the police chief. And like Mr. Rosenberg, Danny was dressed in plaid pajama pants and a waffle knit Henley, better suited to a night of sitting on the couch watching TV, than trying to catch a shooter.

"I never got a look at the person. I guess I just assumed it would be a man. I'm sorry I don't have more to report."

"It's okay, Mr. R." I reached out and patted his hand. "You were very brave to chase him the way you did."

"Or foolish." Mrs. Rosenberg snorted. Her salt and pepper bob swung over her shoulders as she whipped her head around to speak to my mother. "I mean, seriously Becky, what was he thinking?"

"He was thinking about protecting my daughter, so I really can't complain. But I know how frightened you must be." My mother passed the platter of apple cake to Mrs. Rosenberg. "Here, have a piece of cake. Made with apples from the Carlow orchard." A smile flitted across her face as she glanced over at Danny.

His radio squawked. "Your brother is here, Chief, and he's insisting on getting into the house."

"I imagine he is." Danny winked at me. "You can let him up to the house, just be sure he stays on the driveway and doesn't interfere with any potential evidence."

Fluffy had planted herself solidly on top of my feet under the table, but she lifted her head and growled when the front door opened.

"Amanda? Where are you?" Dylan's voice was louder than necessary and shook a tiny bit.

Once she heard her beloved's voice, Fluffy stopped with the growling, rose and trotted happily toward the front hall, with her plumed tail waving over her back.

"We're in the kitchen," I replied.

His footsteps pounded down the hall, but stopped when Fluffy and he met at the kitchen doorway. He scooped Fluffy up, held her tight, and murmured into her fur, "Are your mom and you okay, girl?"

"We are," I answered for Fluffy.

He put her down and rushed to my side. I stood and he pulled me into his arms. "I was never so scared in my life as I was when Rita called to tell me Danny had gotten called out to a shooting at your address."

"Cocoa?" My mom said from behind us.

Dylan released me and reached for the mug. "Thanks, Becky."

"Now I know where I rank in your life... somewhere below hot chocolate."

His lips quirked up and even my toes tingled at the

emotions I saw on his face. "It does have mini marshmal-lows; can you blame me?"

I plopped back in my chair and took a sip of my own drink. "You know, I really can't."

Mr. Rosenberg stood from his seat next to me. "Here, Dylan, take my seat. I'm too wired to sit still anyway."

As Dylan sat and scooted his chair closer to mine, his brother arched an eyebrow at him. "Are you all settled now? May I can continue my investigation?"

"Yes, Chief." Dylan flashed him a saucy salute, which would've gotten anyone besides his baby brother thrown in the slammer.

"Mr. Rosenberg, let's get back to what you could see. Are you able to give us any details about the vehicle the assailant fled in?"

He leaned against the kitchen island and shook his head regretfully. "Not much, I'm sorry. It looked more like a sedan than an SUV or a truck. And it was a dark color, but I couldn't quite make out what it was. Maybe gray, maybe black? It could've even been dark green. If only I'd been faster," he chastised himself.

"If you'd been faster, you might've been shot, and we would know even less than we do now, so stop kicking yourself, sir." Danny's words were harsh, but his tone was gentle.

His chair grated against the tile floor as he pushed it back and rose. "I'm heading back outside. If all of you could stay here until we're done, I'd appreciate it. In case we have more questions."

After he left, Dylan turned to study my face. "You're really okay?"

I reached out and clasped his hand. "I swear, I'm fine. Just shook up."

"Does anyone else think this shooter has to be the person who killed Dennis Millikan?" Dylan asked.

Around the table everyone raised their hands, including me. Heck, if she could, Fluffy probably would've raised her paw. I mean who else would want to shoot me?

"My brother said they located shell casings in the copse of trees where the shooter had been standing. They were 22-caliber long rifle cartridges. So the sort of gun someone would use for hunting small game." Dylan sipped his coffee.

Across the booth from us at the diner the next morning, Cara and Jeremy stared at us with wide eyes and jaws dropped. Their coffees were untouched.

"I can't believe someone tried to kill you last night." Cara reached across the table and squeezed my hand.

"Again," Jeremy added.

"Hey, no one's tried to murder me for months." My attempt at a joke landed with a thud.

"It's not funny," Jeremy said.

"No, but I was trying to lighten the mood."

"I think attempted murder is a mood you can leave heavy," Cara said.

"But I don't think they were trying to kill me. I think they were aiming at Fluffy."

"Why would anyone want to shoot The Beast? I mean, aside from the obvious," Jeremy said.

I leaned back against the red vinyl booth and crossed my arms over my chest. I leveled my gaze at Jeremy. "The obvious?"

He flapped his hands. "How she's the spawn of Satan."

"She is not!" I uncrossed my arms and reached across

the table to swat his hand. "She acts out because of her anxiety issues, but she's a good girl at heart."

"Then why was someone taking potshots at her?" Jeremy asked.

"Because Amanda is getting too close, and Millikan's killer wanted to send her a warning," Dylan ground out.

"Like the horse head in the bed in the old mobster movie?" Cara asked.

"Exactly!" Dylan pointed at her.

"What makes you think they were aiming for The Beast?" Jeremy took a sip of coffee.

"The bullets were low on the tree. At shih tzu height. Fluffy was standing a little to my right, and the shots were going low and to my right. Not at me. But if they were trying to get me to stop investigating, they made a serious mistake. They never should've come for Fluffy, because now I'm more determined than ever to find them and make them pay."

"Now *you* sound like you're in a mob movie," Jeremy said.

"What I don't understand is why they poisoned Millikan, but shot at you. Don't murderers usually stick to the same MO?" Cara said.

"No one but Amanda or Dylan could get close enough to The Beast to poison her," Jeremy answered.

"But she loves food. Someone could put a little poisoned treat somewhere Fluffy could eat it, and she'd gobble it up," Dylan said.

"I think the killer was hoping Millikan's murder would go unnoticed. He wasn't exactly in great shape, and he had serious anger issues. Would anyone really be surprised if he dropped dead of a heart attack? But Danny suspected it was something more. And then when the state police got involved and started looking at Dylan, I began to investigate too." I looked around the table.

"And like I said before, you're getting close," Dylan barked.

A silence fell over the table, and it wasn't one of those comfortable ones that sometimes happen between old friends. Cara and Jeremy exchanged a glance and squirmed in their seats like kids whose parents were fighting. But I didn't want to fight with Dylan. I wanted to clear his name.

"If I'm close, then let's think about the suspects. Which one knows how to shoot and had access to a weapon?" I asked.

Jeremy shrugged. "A twenty-two in Maple Hills? Pretty much everyone could lay their hands on one."

"Okay, then which of our suspects knows how to shoot?"

"Mallory," Cara said.

My mouth formed an 'O', and my eyes bulged like a cartoon character. Probably not my best look, but her answer caught me by surprise.

Dylan snapped his fingers. "You're right. She was a biathlete back in the day. Don't know if she kept up with it, but she was good."

"Biathlete? Is that the sport where people cross-country ski and then shoot at targets?" I squelched a pang of jealousy as I pictured Mallory gliding across the snow on her skis like some Nordic goddess, with her rifle slung over her shoulder and her golden locks flowing behind her. I mean, Dylan picked me, right? Argh. Even this brief time with Mallory dredged up high school insecurities I'd left behind long ago. But sixteen-year-old Amanda needed to stay in the past. I was a confident, successful woman now, and Mallory didn't hold any power over me, unless she was holding a gun on Fluffy and me. Self-confidence didn't stand a chance against a bullet.

"Yep," Cara said. "I think she even qualified to try out for the Olympics when we were in college."

"Mallory is one suspect who had the skills to shoot at me last night." I held up one finger, and then raised the one next to it. "Can we go for two?"

"Hmm ...we don't know enough about the guy from Chicago to know if he can shoot," Cara said.

"Gary Bullaro? I can check with Carol at the Dew Drop Inn to see if he's a hunter. A lot of them stay there during hunting season. I can grab Fluffy and run over there after breakfast."

"Where is The Beast this morning?" Jeremy asked.

"She's home with my mom, who has softened towards her after last night. She even let me leave her loose in the house and not put her in the crate."

"Will wonders never cease?" Cara snorted.

Dylan's gaze was unfocused, and he paid no attention to us. He tapped his index finger on the table. "I remembered something about Bitsy Van Dyke's husband. He was a hunter. My dad was always having to chase him off orchard property. He'd come and take potshots at squirrels with his rifle."

"A twenty-two?" Jeremy asked.

"Maybe. I don't remember. But he's been out of the picture for a long time, and he probably took his guns with him when he left town," Dylan said.

Jeremy pursed his lips. "I just remembered something too. My mom was in a birdwatching club with Bitsy. She used to feel sorry for her, because Mr. Van Dyke fancied himself a real macho outdoorsman. He was always taking Bitsy and Adrian with him on hunting and camping trips. Bitsy liked to look at the birds, not shoot them. And Adrian was just a little kid and wasn't into it either, but it didn't matter to Mr. Van Dyke. He wanted them to hunt too. He was a real bully."

"So she may not have liked it, but there's a good chance Bitsy would know how to handle a weapon." I sat up straight in my seat.

"What about Nesbitt Sharpley-Smythe? He doesn't strike me as a hunter," Cara said.

"No, but he has a place in Litchfield, what do you want to bet he has guns on hand and brings business associates out to the hills to hunt?" Dylan asked.

"It's possible." I bobbed my head. "We'd need to talk to Mallory or him to be sure, though."

"Or he could've hired a pro," Cara suggested.

"A pro wouldn't have missed Fluffy," Jeremy said.

Dylan bobbed his head. "True, and he wouldn't have been using a twenty-two."

Relief washed over me as they debunked the hit man theory. Who wants to think a professional killer was after them?

"Good morning."

I started at the sound of a man's voice at the end of the table. We'd been so focused on our conversation; I hadn't even noticed him approach. I glanced over to see who it was, and my heart sank. "Detective Panchak, I didn't see you come in."

"No, you were very busy talking. It seemed like a really engrossing topic." He stared at each of us in turn.

I squirmed and slanted a glance at Dylan next to me in the booth. How much had Panchak heard? And how much trouble would we be in for continuing to investigate?

We all stayed mum, and Panchak finally broke the silence. "I'm glad I ran into you, Carlow. Save me a trip to the orchard later. I wanted to ask you if you own any weapons. Say a 22-caliber rifle?"

Dylan's leg tensed where it pressed against mine under the table. He clenched his fists, and his nostrils even flared. I don't think I'd ever seen anyone's nostrils flare before. Uh-oh. Dylan didn't lose his temper often, but it seemed Panchak might've pushed him to that point. He stood up, nose to nose with the state police detective.

"Why don't you do what my tax dollars pay you to do, and find Millikan's murderer?"

"It's what I'm trying to do." Panchak took a step back and held up his hands.

"By following me to the diner to ask me about guns? Who's next, Hitch? Why don't you look at some real suspects for a change? There are plenty of them, with motive, means, and opportunity. But as long as you're laser-focused on the wrong people, someone is going to get away with murder."

"Okay, Mr. Carlow let's take it down a notch," Panchak spoke in the reasonable voice he might use in a hostage negotiation.

"Take it down a notch? Please." Dylan shook his head and chuffed out a humorless laugh. "You're practically accusing me of shooting at my girlfriend and her dog last night."

"No one said you—"

Dylan raised his hand and cut Panchak off, "I would never harm a hair on either of their heads. I love them, and they're in danger, because you're too blind to see I would never kill a man. So, why don't you do your job and protect Amanda by finding the real killer, before he harms her or Fluffy?"

Silence fell over the diner as everyone openly gaped at our table. After what seemed like an eternity, but was really just a few seconds, Sunny applauded slowly behind the counter. One by one, the locals in the restaurant stood up and joined her in giving Dylan a standing ovation.

Panchak's face was the color of an October maple leaf as he looked around at the mutiny occurring at the Sunny Side Up Diner. Without another word, he stormed out of the diner. As he slammed the door behind him, the little bell over it jingled in a cheery manner, which must've added insult to injury for Panchak.

Sunny hollered over the applause, "Your breakfast is on the house this morning, Dylan."

Chapter Fifteen

"You want to know if Gary Bullaro has gone hunting while he's here?" Carol stuck out her bottom lip. "Funny you should ask. He did say he wanted to give it a try. Took one of the brochures from the rack over there."

I looked across the lobby of the Dew Drop Inn, which wasn't hard as it was roughly the size of a postage stamp. The décor hadn't been updated since I worked here back in high school, and it was dated even then. Lots of pine paneling, shag carpet in shades of rusts and browns, and opposite me was a rack of brochures of local attractions.

Two steps took me to the rack, and a colorful one caught my eye. It wasn't anything to do with hunting, but nostalgia washed over me like hot cocoa, and I pulled it out first. "Santa's Christmas Village! I used to look forward to it all year. Is it too early to be excited for the holidays?"

Carol snorted. "Since it's not even Halloween yet, I'd say so. But to tell you the truth, I am too."

"The town green always looks so pretty decked out for the holidays. With the big Christmas tree and giant light up menorah." I flicked through the brochure and gasped with pleasure. "They still do Santa's sleigh rides! I can't wait."

"First we just have to get through leaf-peeping season. Things still busy at the orchard?"

"Unbelievably busy. I don't know how Dylan does it. And all while he's being suspected of murder."

"Ridiculous. But the detective must be widening his search, because he told Gary Bullaro not to leave the area. So he's taken his room indefinitely. Not that I mind, he's quiet and keeps to himself, but he's not happy about it. He wants out of Maple Hills in the worst way."

"Interesting." I tapped the holiday brochure against my chin. "Do you think he's anxious to get away because he's guilty and wants to put some distance between him and the crime scene?"

Carol shrugged. "Maybe. Or maybe he's just a city boy and is bored out of his gourd here. That's why he was asking what there was to do in town. Nothing on the brochure rack appealed to him, until he found the one on local hunting."

I peered at the rack until I found the one Carol was talking about and pulled it out of its slot. "Is he a hunter? Surprising, since he's such a city person."

"He didn't seem to know much about hunting, but said he was going to look into it." She shook her head and tsked her tongue. "It makes you worry about walking in the woods when you see people with no clue what they're doing so eager to grab a gun and shoot at stuff."

"Did he have his own hunting rifle?" I asked.

"Definitely not. He asked where he could get all the gear, including a gun. Why are you asking about guns? Millikan was poisoned, wasn't he?"

"He was, but someone shot at Fluffy and me last night."

Her gaze focused on me like a laser, and she drew in a sharp breath. "What?"

"I can't believe you haven't heard yet. Usually you don't miss a trick."

"It's been so busy; I've been here day and night lately. Are you okay? Is The Beast all right?"

"We're both fine."

She exhaled with a whoosh. "Thank heavens. Where were you when it happened?"

"My parents' front yard."

"What?" Carol shouted. "Be careful. You must be getting close, kiddo."

I shook my head slowly side to side. "It seems like it, but the truth is, Carol, suspects are thick on the ground. I'm nowhere near close to solving the mystery."

"You must be closer than you think. Why else would someone take potshots at you and The Beast?"

A CAR CRUNCHED OVER THE GRAVEL PARKING LOT FOR THE orchard shop, and I tugged Fluffy reluctantly away from the tire of a car with North Carolina plates. More out-of-towners here for an authentic New England autumn experience. "Enough sniffing, Fluff. I've got to get you settled in at Dylan's house now, or I'm going to be late for my shift."

"If you're sleeping with the boss, is being late really a problem?" A woman's voice sounded from behind us.

I recognized the unpleasant tone, and shut my eyes for a moment. "Hello, Mallory. I don't know, maybe you could tell me?"

"You—" She narrowed her glittering sapphire blue eyes at me and hissed out the word.

Fluffy cut her off by barking ferociously and charging

toward her. I gripped her leash, so she couldn't advance and turned to face my former classmate. "Enough."

"Good, you're finally keeping your little monster in check."

"I meant enough from you. Can't we drop all the antagonism? We're grown women now, not high schoolers anymore."

"But I still look like this," She swept one hand along her slender, model-like figure, which was on full display in a fitted dress and heels that made her mile-long legs look more like two miles. She sneered and continued, "And you still look like that."

I refused to take the bait. "Exactly the kind of thing I meant. Yes, you were the queen of the high school, and I was a lowly nerd. Get over it. Why can't we be civil to each other now?"

Fluffy had stopped barking, but kept a wary eye on Mallory, and I knew I couldn't ease up my grip or she'd make her move.

"I just don't understand why Dylan has chosen you instead of me."

"And I don't understand why you care? It's obvious you're with Nesbitt Sharpley-Smythe. Why are you still so determined to pursue Dylan? Is it to get one over on me? If so, I understand your motives even less. We haven't seen each other in going on twenty years, why would you still be so invested in hating me?"

"You don't understand."

"Then explain it to me."

She put her hands on her hips and snapped, "Because Nesbitt has been very clear. I need to do whatever it takes to get Dylan to sell his land." She paused and then added meaningfully, "Whatever. It. Takes."

Realization dawned, and my eyes widened. My grip

slackened on the leash, and Fluffy immediately took advantage of the situation and advanced. Mallory took a step back, and I regained my composure and tightened the leash. "You mean Nesbitt has told you to make a play for Dylan to get him to agree, even though you two are a couple?"

"You might've lived in big cities since you left Maple Hills, but you're still very provincial, aren't you?" Her lips twisted up and she snorted ever-so-delicately. "Nesbitt and I have a very sophisticated relationship."

"And by sophisticated, you mean he's willing to trade you for several hundred acres of land to develop? If that's what you mean by sophisticated, then I'm happy to be provincial."

"Whatever. I just can't believe Dylan is passing up his chance with me, to stay true to you."

"Then you don't know him at all. He's one of the most honorable men I've ever met. Unlike Nesbitt." My heart stopped for a moment as the realization struck me that maybe what Mallory meant by 'whatever it takes' was murdering Millikan and setting Dylan up for the crime to get his land.

"Honor doesn't earn you the big bucks."

No, but it allows you to keep your soul. I caught myself before I spoke the words aloud. I wanted to get a little more information from Mallory, and if we kept sparring I would blow my chance. "Valid point."

Her brow would've furrowed if it hadn't been frozen by cosmetic procedures. My reasonable reply threw her off balance. "Thank you?"

I kicked a piece of gravel and kept my tone light. "So what are you two sophisticates doing for fun in Maple Hills while you're stuck here?"

Mallory eyed me through slanted eyes. After a couple

of seconds, she decided to try for a more friendly approach too. Did it mean there was a human soul buried deep inside her, or was she lulling me into a false sense of security to strike later? "There's not much to do. If it were winter, I could hit the trails and cross-country ski."

"Right, you did biathlon in high school."

"I still do. I love it. Nothing like being outside in the winter, gliding along on skis—"

"And shooting at stuff?" I interrupted.

"At targets. I don't shoot at animals. Although I might make an exception for this little rat." She mimed a kick in Fluffy's general direction, and was rewarded with a fierce growl.

"Interesting. Because last night, someone did shoot at Fluffy and me."

Her jaw slackened. "And you think it was me?"

I shrugged. "Maybe. You did just admit you wanted to shoot my dog."

"That was just talk. I wouldn't really do it." Her words tumbled out, and she held up her hands.

"Even if I'm in the way of your attempts to seduce Dylan and get him under your sway?"

She chuffed out a derisive laugh. "Mallory Davisson has never in her life had to kill a woman to get a man."

"How about Nesbitt? Does he hunt?"

She pursed her scarlet lips. "He does on occasion, but he doesn't really enjoy it. He brings potential business partners to his home in Litchfield to do all the outdoorsy things. Hunting, fishing. But he didn't shoot at you last night either."

"If he has access to hunting rifles at his home a few towns away, how can you be so sure?"

"Because we were together." She jutted out her chin. "We can alibi each other. We were together from dinner last night until breakfast this morning. Now, if you're done accusing me of crimes, I have an appointment with Dylan."

She pivoted and tried to storm off across the parking lot, but her whisper-thin heel caught on the gravel and her ankle twisted. With a huff, she straightened up and proceeded more cautiously toward the office.

I scooped up Fluffy and looked into her dark brown eyes. "I don't know, Fluff. Her alibi doesn't hold much weight with me. I mean Nesbitt and Mallory have proven they have no sense of honor. Both of them would be willing to lie to cover up for the other. Do you think one of them was the shooter? And if so, does it mean they're also the murderer?"

"THANKS AGAIN, ERIC. YOU'RE THE BEST." I SHUT THE door to his home office behind me with one hand and held onto Fluffy with the other.

Jeremy and his husband lived in a Victorian home, which they picked up for a song because it was in disrepair. They'd been painstakingly renovating it as time allowed, but Eric's office for his graphic arts business on the top floor was one of the first areas they completed. I carried Fluffy down the narrow stairs and my other hand held onto the railing with a death grip.

As I neared the ground floor, my best friend's voice greeted me. "Hi, Amanda." Waiting at the bottom of the stairs, still dressed for work, Jeremy held two glasses of red wine. He shoved one toward me. I put Fluffy down and grabbed the glass from him. My dog and Jeremy gave each other some serious side-eye but seemed to have reached an uneasy truce.

We clinked glasses and gave our usual toast, since we started doing it with juice boxes as kids, "*Tous pour un, un pour tous!*"

After taking a sip, Jeremy waved his hand toward the living room. "I started a fire. Let's go sit in there while we have our wine."

The smoky scent of the burning logs warmed my spirit as well as my toes, and I plopped in an armchair by the fireplace. Jeremy took the chair opposite and Fluffy planted herself in front of the hearth between us.

"Eric wanted me to tell you he's going to start working on my cover while his ideas are fresh. He'll be down in a little while." I took a sip of my wine.

"I take it your meeting went well then?" Jeremy arched one brow.

I nodded eagerly and sat on the edge of my seat. "It did. So well. Eric is an amazing artist. I showed him the covers of bestselling novels in the historical mystery genre, so he could see what was moving books right now, and we reviewed the forms about my book he'd asked me to fill out in advance. We talked about what I liked and his vision for the cover, and he dove right into it." I bounced on my seat. "This is really happening, Jer. I'm about to publish my first novel."

"And it's so good. You're going to be on bestseller lists before you know it."

"Doubtful. It's a tough business and super-competitive, but it's a start."

"And I remember when we used to hang around the library after school, and you would show me where your books would go on the shelves when you were a published author. I'm so proud of you for making it happen."

My face heated, and I couldn't blame the warmth of the cozy fire. "It means so much to me to be doing this all back in Maple Hills. And that you edited the manuscript for me and Eric is doing the cover art."

"We're all so happy you're home, just do us all a favor and try not to get yourself killed. We'd miss you even more now that we've gotten used to having you around again. Besides, who would take care of The Beast if anything happened to you?"

"I'm convinced the shooter last night was aiming at Fluffy, not me. Which infuriates me to no end. Who would hurt a harmless creature?"

Jeremy crossed his legs, leaned back in his chair, and cast a skeptical gaze in Fluffy's direction. "Creature, I'll give you. But harmless? The Beast?"

"Mallory expressed a desire to shoot Fluffy today," I announced.

"I wish I could pretend to be surprised, but seriously, Amanda, The Beast can be a monster. And so is Mallory. Put them together, and it's a combustible situation. Where did you see Mallory today?"

I recounted the story of our meeting.

Jeremy audibly gasped when I was done. "Nesbitt is her lover, and he wants to hand her over to Dylan as a way to seal his real estate deal? It's just... " He flapped his hands, while he searched for the right word to describe the situation.

"Ishy?" I suggested.

"Ishy to the max. Who does that? The rich really are different, aren't they?"

"My grandfather used to say anyone could be rich if money was all that mattered to them, and until I met Nesbitt I never really understood. But, if the almighty dollar is all you care about—not your relationships with people, or the state of the world, morals, love—then you'll achieve your goal, because nothing will stop you."

Jeremy nodded and took a sip of his wine. "I see what you mean. Without a pesky moral compass you'd do anything to get money. Including making your girlfriend come on to another man."

"Ishy," I reiterated. After a pause, I continued, "And it might be even worse. What if they murdered Millikan as a way to set up Dylan to be arrested, so they could get their hands on his land?"

He sat up ramrod straight and stared at me with wide eyes. "Would even they do something that twisted?'

"If twisted was a business, they would be the chairman and the CEO. Seriously, they are one freaky couple. I wouldn't put anything past them."

"So, do you think they shot at you?"

"They could have. I certainly take their alibi of each other with a grain of salt, they both lie as naturally as they breathe. But they're not the only suspects. Bullaro was asking Carol about hunting while he was stuck here in town. It might've been an excuse for him to ask where he could buy a rifle to shoot at Fluffy and me."

"And don't forget Bitsy Van Dyke. Have you talked to her yet?"

"I haven't had a chance. I've been on the move since breakfast this morning. Hopefully, tomorrow, I can talk to her."

He shook his head. "I'm not sure I can see Bitsy killing someone. She's so fluttery. I always assumed she was mild mannered."

"Still waters run deep, especially where a woman's only child is concerned."

"She *is* obsessed with Adrian, especially since his accident. And because he lost his license as a result of the DUI, he's completely dependent on her for transportation."

"Which would have to be hard for a young man. At that age, you want to break out on your own, not spend every waking minute with your mom." I rested my head against the chair and gazed at the flickering flames. The dancing orange fire mesmerized me, until an idea struck me, and I sat up straight. "You mean Adrian doesn't drive for legal reasons, not because of his physical limitations?"

"Could be a little of both. Why?" Jeremy stretched his legs out, and propped his stocking feet up on the bluestone hearth.

"I'm not sure. I'd just assumed he was dependent on Bitsy because he was incapable of living on his own." I raised one shoulder and let it fall. "It might not mean anything, but it's interesting."

Jeremy inclined his head. "Their whole dynamic is interesting, in a gothic novel kind of way. Adrian is Bitsy's everything. I have to be honest, she acts like she's furious at Millikan about the accident, but there's a tiny voice in the back of my mind saying maybe she's happy about it because it's made Adrian as physically dependent on her as she is emotionally dependent on him."

I bit by bottom lip. Jeremy had good instincts, so if they were telling him Bitsy might not really be sorry about Adrian's condition, it raised a question in my mind. "If Bitsy is happy about taking care of Adrian, would she really want to kill Millikan, or does it take away her motive?"

Chapter Sixteen

With the house to myself the next morning, I decided to tackle the process of putting my book up for preorder on the online retailers. A huge learning curve, and I was glad for the peace and quiet to figure it all out before my afternoon shift at the orchard. Dressed in yoga pants and an oversized sweatshirt with a cup of much-needed coffee, and Fluffy snoozing at my feet, I was prepared to drill down into my work.

After a few minutes, my phone pinged as my parents' smart home device's cheery voice chirped, "Someone is at the door."

I glanced at the app on my phone to see the front doorbell camera. Who could it be on a weekday morning at ten o'clock? My heart sank to my fuzzy slippers. Nesbitt Sharpley-Smythe. What in the ever-loving world was he doing on our doorstep? I briefly toyed with the idea of pretending I wasn't home, when he pounded on the door. Impatient much? This time, Fluffy roused from her slumber and ran to the door like a little big shot, barking furiously.

Looked like my plan to hunker down and pretend the house was empty was shot all to heck. I heaved a deep sigh and stood. My slippers scuffed along the hardwood floors as I dragged myself down the hallway from the kitchen to the entryway. Maybe if I took long enough, he'd give up and leave.

Once there, I allowed myself one deep breath before I pasted a smile on my face, picked up Fluffy, and threw open the door. "Mr. Sharpley-Smythe, what a surprise."

His eyebrows raised ever so slightly as his gaze travelled down my body, taking in my eccentric outfit. Hey, show up uninvited at someone's house before eleven in the morning, and you get what you get.

"I can see I caught you by surprise. I'm sorry, but I wanted to catch you before you left for work."

Fluffy continued to bark, while I pondered what the man might want to see me about so urgently. He cleared his throat. Evidently, I paused too long, but I hadn't finished my coffee yet, and I wasn't firing on all cylinders.

"May I come inside?"

I stepped aside and waved my left arm. "Of course."

Seeing the person she viewed as intruder entering our home whipped Fluffy into a frenzy. Her barking grew more shrill, and my ears tingled a bit at the piercing sound so close to them, as I clutched the squirming dog in my right arm.

"Hush, Fluff," I murmured as I shut the door. He cast an expectant glance my way. Right. Social niceties. "Would you like a cup of coffee? I just made a pot."

"Coffee would be lovely, thank you."

"Please, follow me." I put Fluffy down and led my unwanted guest to the kitchen. Fluffy stuck close to my side and kept a wary eye on Sharpley-Smythe. "Have a seat. How do you take your coffee?"

"Black."

I grabbed a mug and poured him a cup. When I turned around, I noticed he was still standing as he stared at the messy kitchen table. My laptop sat open at the seat at the head of the table, and my notebooks, binders, and research materials were strewn across half of it.

"Sorry about the mess. I was working." I handed him the cup of coffee, and straightened things into neat-ish piles.

He sat at the seat to my left, which afforded him a lovely view out the bank of windows overlooking the backyard and pond. "Ah, yes. I'd heard you're writing a book."

"I am. It's why I moved back to Maple Hills."

"And prior to that, you were a VP of Human Resources for a very large company in Los Angeles. Very impressive career trajectory for a woman of your age."

While it was true most people in my former professional position were older than I was, my jaw clenched at his words. The man had done his homework on me. Why? Having someone as ruthless as Nesbitt Sharpley-Smythe taking an intense interest in my life chilled me to my core.

I decided to put him on the defensive, since he'd clearly been trying to throw me off my game. I leaned back in my chair, and forced my jaw to loosen. "You've certainly had your people researching me. Which begs the question ... why?"

His eyes widened fractionally, but it was his only tell I'd taken him by surprise. He shifted his glance to look outside, and gestured to the window with his coffee mug. "Your parents have a lovely view."

"For now," I said in a pointed manner.

"Whatever do you mean? Are they moving?" He shifted his gaze to study my face.

"No, but if you get your way, the view will change

dramatically. Those apple trees on the other side of the pond are Dylan's orchard. I imagine the noise during construction will be unbearable, and the view once it's complete will be significantly less scenic."

He chuckled. "My, you don't mince words, do you?"

"Out of curiosity, what will be over there if your plan comes to pass?"

His gaze grew unfocused as he looked out the window, as if he were seeing his development in his mind's eye. "That area will be housing units. Apartments, all with balconies to maximize the view of the pond."

I narrowed my eyes. "How many housing units in total are we talking here?"

He raised one shoulder and let it fall in a graceful manner. "Enough."

"Enough for a cozy community, or enough for an infantry division?"

"Both of those options would be too small for my vision.'

My heart raced. Just how big was this development, and how did he expect Maple Hills current infrastructure to support it? "Where would all those people work? And shop? In case it's escaped your attention, Maple Hills is a tiny town in the middle of nowhere."

He put his cup down and steepled his fingers. "The project is much larger than the public realizes. We've attracted corporations to invest in manufacturing facilities here, as well as office buildings. Also retail outlets, restaurants, everything we'd need to support the booming population."

I couldn't maintain my neutral expression, and my eyes bugged out of my head. "Who knows the extent of your plan?" It was beyond belief the First Selectman of our town knew all this and was on board. Factories? Malls?

Blocks of apartment buildings? It would change everything that made Maple Hills, well, Maple Hills. All the quaint, New England charm would be gone.

"Outside of my inner circle, very few people. Unfortunately for me, Dennis Millikan was one of them."

"Millikan knew? Why?" My mind raced as I tried to figure out why a low-level blowhard would be one of the select group aware of the extent of the development.

"He was helping me."

"Helping you how?" Suspicion dripped from my voice.

"I told you once before. He was helping me convince Dylan Carlow to sell."

"Torpedoing Dylan's hard cider venture wouldn't be enough to force Dylan to sell his land. Did you have some other scheme for Millikan to influence Dylan's decision? They were hardly friends. He wouldn't have been able to convince Dylan to sell his family's land."

"It was a miscalculation on my part. A rare occurrence, but it does happen. You see, my dear, I'd assumed the orchard was in financial trouble when Carlow branched off into the cider business, and he needed the money the cider would bring in to succeed to stay afloat. If Millikan had been able to sabotage his efforts, than Carlow would've been forced to sell the land to me."

"But the cider venture is just to provide a less seasonal income stream. The success of the entire orchard is not dependent upon it."

"Hence, my error in judgement. And, even if I had been correct, Millikan made no headway in obliterating the cider business. I also ignored Mallory's knowledge of the town and underestimated the amount of loyalty the community would give to a local over a newcomer. This project has not been my most shining hour professionally."

The gears in my mind all clicked into place with a solid

kerchunk. "So Millikan knew the extent of your plans. *That's* what he was blackmailing you about, not your relationship with Mallory."

"You are a very bright woman. If being an author doesn't work out for you, I would love the opportunity to find a place for you in my organization."

Unease skittered up my spine. Why was he admitting all these top-secret things to me now? Was Sharpley-Smythe behind the murder and intended me to be his next victim?

But, wait, he'd just kinda-sorta offered me a job, and he wouldn't do so if he was planning to kill me in my parents' kitchen. I decided to once again go on the conversational offensive. "Why are you admitting all of this to me?"

My blunt words caused an unexpected reaction. He threw back his head and roared with laughter, perhaps the first genuine emotion I'd seen the man show since I'd met him. "Working with you would be very amusing and would have the added benefit of annoying Mallory to no end. Since I'm a little irritated with her at the moment, please do consider my offer."

I leaned back and folded my arms across my chest. Of course, with the cartoonish image of a shih-tzu on my baggy sweatshirt, it probably wasn't the intimidating look I was going for. "I notice you dodged my question. Why are you telling me all this hush-hush information? If I accepted your offer, would my job duties include convincing Dylan to sell his land to you?"

He waved one long-fingered hand gracefully in the air. "No, no. I'm afraid that ship has sailed. I'm able to tell you details of the project now, because Maple Hills is off the table. I have my team trying to find another location for our development. One more amenable to our plans." The corners of his lips tilted up slightly. "I'll do you the favor of being as blunt with you as you've been with me. I have the uneasy feeling you suspect me of killing Millikan and shooting at you and your—" he paused and sneered down at Fluffy, who returned the gaze with a baring of her sharp, little teeth. "—*delightful* canine companion. I wanted to disabuse you of those notions."

"And how precisely, do you think our conversation this morning has allayed my suspicions in any way, shape, or form?" After the incredulous words tumbled from my lips, I wished I could suck them back into my mouth. What was I thinking poking a potentially murderous bear this way?

"I'd hoped once you heard I was abandoning the Carlow land development plan, you'd realize I hadn't killed anyone."

My phone pinged at the moment the front door opened and my dad's voice boomed down the hall, "I'm home from cardiac rehab, sweetie."

Fluffy ran out from under the table and barked in greeting, which to the uninitiated sounded a lot like her threatening bark. I glanced at Sharpley-Smythe who recoiled slightly as she brushed past his trouser leg, and then rose.

"We're in the kitchen, Dad."

It looked like my meeting with Nesbitt Sharpley-Smythe had come to an abrupt conclusion. Unfortunately for him, it had done nothing to convince me he wasn't the murderer. Just because he was being forced to abandon his plans for Maple Hills now, doesn't mean he wouldn't have been willing to kill to hold onto them a week ago.

The only other time I'd been happier to see my father was in the ICU after his open-heart surgery. Because a part of me wondered if his arrival had done more than spare me from an uncomfortable conversation. Had my dad just saved Fluffy and me from falling to the same fate as Dennis Millikan?

UNABLE TO COME DOWN FROM MY ADRENALINE RUSH AFTER Sharpley-Smythe left, focusing on the technical details of my book's preorder was impossible. I finally gave up, showered, and brought Fluffy to Dylan's house before my shift.

Which is how I now found myself exiting the Sit and Sip with a cardboard tray full of caffeinated beverages for my co-workers and me. The ice cubes in the iced coffee rattled together, and I pondered with my nerves still on edge, perhaps the mega hazelnut latte I'd purchased for myself might not have been the best plan.

I bumped the door open with my hip and spun right into the burly chest of a man entering the coffee shop. "Sorry, I wasn't looking."

"No problem, miss. Hey, I know you," the man said.

With my back still propping the door open, I looked up at his face. "Mr. Bullaro, hello."

"Amelia, right?" He furrowed his brow.

"Amanda."

"Right, right."

I knew I should step out of his way and let him enter, but the sleuthing gods had put him in my path at just the right moment, and I wasn't about to let the opportunity to question him about hunting rifles slip away. "How much longer will you be staying in our fair town?"

He scowled. "Until the police say I can leave. Which is ridiculous, just because I came here to see Dennis, doesn't mean I killed him."

"Of course not." I schooled my expression into what I hoped was sympathetic understanding, but given my current state of agitation, it probably looked more like manic anxiety.

"And with all due respect to your town, Amanda, there isn't much to do in this backwater."

Right, because calling the town a backwater was the ultimate in respect. But to lure him into answering my questions, I needed to keep things amiable. "There are only so many leaves you can peep at, am I right?" I grinned.

Gary laughed. A deep, hearty sound. "You ain't wrong."

"There are other things to do in town."

"Oh, yeah? Name 'em," he challenged.

"Lots of people come for fishing and hunting. Are you a sportsman, Mr. Bullaro?"

"Call me Gary, and no I'm not. I'm a city boy, born and bred. Fishing seems like a big snore to me, but I thought I might give hunting a try. Even went to a sporting goods store the broad who runs the Dew Drop recommended."

The thought flashed in my mind Carol wouldn't be thrilled to be called a broad, but then I remembered the times I'd heard her refer to herself as one, and smothered a smile. "How did it go? Did you ... um..." I stumbled over the right word here. Did you say shoot? Kill? I decided on a less bloodthirsty word, since he was a murder suspect. "...hunt anything?"

"Nah." He waved his hands. "I decided not to do it. What do I want to kill an animal for? It's not like I need them for meat or anything. It just seemed pointless to me."

"So, you didn't buy any hunting equipment. Like a rifle?"

He frowned, and I realized the question might've been

a little too pointed. Sharpley-Smythe had called me blunt this morning, and perhaps he was right.

"What would be the point of buying a hunting rifle if I didn't want to go hunting?"

I shrugged and widened my eyes in a disingenuous manner. "Perhaps you wanted to shoot at something else?"

"Like what?" He narrowed his eyes and pursed his lips.

"Um ... me?" I suggested in a weak voice.

"You? Why in the blue blazes would I want to shoot at a pretty, young woman like you? What are you talking about here?"

"Someone took a pot shot at my dog and me the other night—"

"And you thought it was *me*?" He raised his voice, and conversation in the Sit and Sip came to a sudden halt.

"Maybe?" I shrugged. And as his face reddened to match the brick building we were in, I rushed to add, "But probably not. Almost certainly not. I mean, why would you?"

"Why do you think I did? What made you think of me in the first place?" He lowered his voice, and sounded genuinely puzzled.

"The police are investigating my boyfriend for Millikan's murder too, and I know he didn't do it. But if they're focused on him, it means they're not looking for the real killer. So, I've been poking around, trying to see what I could learn."

"You've gone rogue and are investigating on your own?" He whistled between his teeth. "You're either gutsy or stupid."

I held my thumb and forefinger a smidgeon apart. "Maybe a little of both?"

He bobbed his head. "You must be getting close if someone took a shot at you."

"That's the general consensus."

"But it wasn't me." And on that closing salvo, he brushed past me to enter the coffee shop.

And here's the thing, after talking to him just now, I was inclined to believe him. But someone had killed Millikan and shot at Fluffy and me, and while my morning interaction with Sharpley-Smythe hadn't removed him from my suspect list, this conversation had moved Gary Bullaro closer to the bottom of it.

Not as low as Hitch and Dylan were, but pretty close. He was brusque and abrasive, but there was also something a little charming about the man. Maybe because he came across as authentically himself. No airs or false graces. Gary Bullaro was who he was. And I was less inclined to think who he was, was a murderer.

But if it wasn't him, who was it? The killer might think I'm getting close, but in my own mind, I was totally at sea.

Chapter Seventeen

"Eric told me he emailed his cover design to you. Do you like it?" Jeremy sat across my parents' kitchen table from me. After my short work shift at the orchard, I'd hoped to do more research on how to format my book, but my work had been interrupted again when Jeremy showed up unannounced.

"No."

He gasped. "You don't?"

"No, I *love* it!"

"You are a cruel woman." He reached over and swatted at my hand.

My dad strolled into the kitchen to refill his water glass from the dispenser on the fridge. "Are you torturing Jeremy again, pumpkin?"

"She is, Mr. Seldon."

"I'm just teasing him a little." We spoke at the same time.

Dad grabbed an apple from the fruit bowl and polished it against his shirt. "Since your mother isn't home to tell me not to encourage you, I have to ask ... do you have any leads on the Millikan murder or who shot at you?"

My mother disapproved of my sleuthing, and while it was turning out to be a dangerous hobby, I couldn't look the other way when someone was being falsely accused. Especially if the someone under suspicion was me, as it was last summer, or Dylan, as was the case right now.

"I'm starting to think it wasn't Gary Bullaro."

"The guy from Illinois? I would've thought he was a hot prospect." Dad bit into the crisp apple with a loud crunch.

"He certainly had motive, and coming all the way here to confront Millikan is suspicious, but I talked to him yesterday, and he doesn't have a gun."

"If you can believe what he said," Jeremy cautioned.

"My instincts were telling me he wasn't lying. And I wasn't getting a murder-y vibe from him."

"Assuming the person who shot at you and Fluffy is also the murderer—"

I cut off my dad, "It must be. Who else would want to shoot us?"

Jeremy snickered. "I have a list, let me just call it up on my phone."

"Hardy-har-har. Seriously, it has to be the same person." Now it was my turn to swat at Jeremy's hand, when he tapped on his phone and pretended to call up a note of potential people who had it in for me. I had friends in Los Angeles, but none like Cara and Jeremy. We had a serious brother-sister thing happening between us, and being an only child, I loved it. Even the teasing.

Dad pointed his apple at me. "Which other suspects have guns?"

"All of them," Jeremy replied.

"We don't know that yet." I held up my index finger.

"Right. You haven't talked to Bitsy yet." Jeremy bobbed his head.

"Bitsy? Why don't you run over to her place right now and see what you can find out?" Dad suggested.

I screwed up my mouth. "It's not a bad idea. If for no other reason than to eliminate her. And I am working at the orchard's Fall Festival booth tonight and tomorrow, so I won't be able to do it for a couple of days if I don't do it now." I looked at Jeremy, "What do you say to a field trip?"

"I'm in!" He replied with alacrity.

His eager tone must've alerted Fluffy to possible action, because she jumped up from where she'd been sleeping in a pool of sunshine on the floor and barked.

"Leave The Beast with me," Dad offered.

"Seriously?" Jeremy's eyes widened.

"Sure, the two of us are forming a sort of nervous bond since the shooting. We'll be fine for an hour or so."

"Thanks, Dad. Let me just put on some shoes, grab my purse and keys, and we'll go." I pressed a quick kiss to Dad's cheek as I passed him on the way out of the room.

"And consider running a comb through your hair. Just sayin'," Jeremy called after me.

Oddly, my heart warmed at his comment. Like I said, being back home with my family and friends made me happy, even when they made rude jokes at my expense. I glanced into the mirror in the hallway, and ran my hands through my messy hair. Although, in this instance, Jeremy had a valid point, but he would never hear it from me.

"MR. PATTERSON, WHAT ARE YOU DOING HERE?"

The young man who answered the door at Bitsy's house

was the one I'd seen at the library the other day. Dressed in sweats, his dark hair was a tumbled mop. He leaned on a cane, and he might've been kind of cute, if not for the unattractive way his mouth hung open as he gaped at his former teacher.

"I'm not here to take back your diploma or anything, so no worries." Jeremy flashed an easy grin at Adrian.

"That's good, since I had a couple of years at college under my belt before this." He waggled his cane.

"We're actually here to see your mom, if she's home," I said.

He cast a quizzical glance my way.

"Amanda, this is Adrian Van Dyke. Adrian, this is my old friend, Amanda Seldon."

"Old?" I nudged Jeremy's arm, and my friend just chuckled in response.

Our kidding seemed to ease the tension in Adrian's shoulders, and he stepped back from the front door. "C'mon in."

As we entered the small Cape Cod-style house, he bellowed, "Mom! Mr. Patterson and Ms. Seldon are here to see you."

Adrian limped into the living room ahead of us and flopped onto a recliner, which appeared to be the only comfortable chair in the room. The rest was antique and looked like it was stuffed with rocks and upholstered with chintz.

"I'll be down in a minute. I just need to finish one thing." Bitsy's voice held an uncertain tone, and there was a slight quaver in it as she called down the stairs.

"No rush, Bitsy." Jeremy paused and said at the bottom of the stairs before joining us in the living room.

I perched on one end of a sofa, and Jeremy sat next to me. The fragile piece of furniture creaked under his weight, and he scooted to the edge. "So Adrian, when can you head back to college?"

"I was hoping I could go back next semester, but Mom insists I stay home again." Adrian pouted.

"Too bad, but your health and well-being have to come first," Jeremy said.

"I know, I know." Adrian rolled his eyes and scowled. "Mom sings that song a hundred times a day."

"It must be rough for you," I said with a sympathetic moue.

He turned his gaze to me and nodded earnestly. "It really is. There's this group of guys I hang out with, from the science department. We all met at orientation and pledged the same fraternity. Study hard and party harder is our motto."

Jeremy pointed his thumb my way. "We have a motto too. *Tous pour un, un pour tous.*"

Adrian's brows met over his eyes. "What does that mean?"

"One for all, and all for one. It's from *The Three Muske-teers*," I said.

"But there are only two of you."

"Cara Diamond is the third." I smiled at Adrian, in spite of the sullen frown on his face.

"You guys get it then; how important friends are. I mean if I don't go back for the spring semester, I can't graduate with the guys. It's killing me."

I wasn't sure how to respond, those college friendships are intense, but once you're out and go your separate ways, you drift apart. At least, it's what happened to me. But, if someone had told me that when I was twenty-one it just would've ticked me off, and I wouldn't have believed them. Footsteps on the stairs saved me from figuring out what to say.

Bitsy scurried to the living room and raked her hands through her hair. "May I get you something to drink? We have some lovely cider from the Maple Hills Orchard. I picked it up at the Fall Festival this morning."

"No thank you." I held up my hands and smiled at her. "Working at the orchard store this season, I've had enough apple-based products to last me until next fall."

"Nothing for me either," said Jeremy. "We're hoping not to take up too much of your time."

She perched on a wingback chair across from the sofa. "I have to admit, I don't have much time to spare. The First Selectman is sending me to a training session for town clerks. A car is picking me up to take me to the airport in a couple of hours. It's why I went to the festival this morning instead of tonight for the fireworks. I'll be sorry to miss them." She drew in a deep breath. Bitsy's conversational style could best be described as rambling. Long sentences tumbled out without pausing, even for breath.

"I'm working at the orchard's booth tonight. I'm hoping to sneak away to hit some of the other attractions," I said.

"Since you're dating the boss, I'm sure it won't be a problem." Jeremy snickered.

Bitsy clasped her hands together until her knuckles whitened and looked at us. "What can I do for you both?"

We'd worked out a plan on the drive over, but I wasn't really feeling it. There was no way to launch into our questions without Bitsy realizing we suspected her of, at best, taking potshots at Fluffy and me, and, at worst, of murdering Dennis Millikan. And if she was innocent, I would have insulted someone I had to face around town. Falsely accusing a neighbor of murder was an irreparable breach.

At my hesitation, Jeremy jumped in and said, "I'm sure

you heard someone shot at Amanda and The Beast the other night."

"The Beast?" Adrian cocked his head.

"Fluffy. My dog. Jeremy thinks he's funny by calling her a rude nickname."

"I had heard some talk about it. I'm very sorry, dear. Are you all right?" Bitsy asked with concern.

"Yes, luckily the person didn't hit us, although an oak tree in my parents' front yard took some damage."

"Oh, what a shame, they have some lovely, old growth trees on their property." Bitsy wrung her hands together. "But I must say, I don't understand why you want to talk to me about it."

Here was the tricky part. How to get Bitsy to talk while basically accusing her of multiple felonies? I took a deep breath and launched into what I hoped was the least offensive way to glean the information we needed. "We suspect the person who shot at us is also the same person who killed Millikan."

"Still not seeing what this has to do with my mom," Adrian said.

"Right, you see, since Chief Carlow had to recuse himself from the case, the state police have taken over, and they seem to be concentrating their attention on local people," I said.

Jeremy bobbed his head. "Like Dylan and Hitch, and ... well, I'm sorry to say, even you, Bitsy."

Her face paled, and she fiddled with the collar of her blouse. "I know. The reason the detective questioned me about it was because I had issues with that horrible man."

Maybe this common ground was a chance to build some rapport between Bitsy and me. "Which is no fun. It happened to me last summer with that murder at the Theater in the Pines, and it's terrifying. It's why we'd like to help clear some of the locals, so the detective can focus on the real culprit, whoever it might be." I resisted the urge to cross my fingers as I told my little lie.

"How very brave of you both. And you must be getting very close if someone is shooting at you and your darling little dog. And heaven knows, it was a terribly unpleasant experience, and if there's anything I can do to never have to be interrogated again, I would be happy to help." Bitsy gasped in a breath at the end of her soliloquy.

"Millikan was poisoned, so we can't really trace the killer through that method. But guns are identifiable. If we could find the one that shot at me, I believe it would lead us to Millikan's murderer, and Dylan, Hitch, and you would be in the clear. I can't imagine a lady like you hunts, so we thought if we could let the police know you don't have a hunting rifle in the house, you'd be off the hook." My pulse thudded strongly in my wrists, but I forced what I hoped was a friendly smile to my lips. If this woman was a killer, I didn't want to put myself back in her crosshairs.

"You're absolutely right, I am not a hunter. But Adrian's father was an avid outdoorsman. Camping, hunting, fishing. He loved it all. Was never happier than when he was traipsing around in the woods with a gun, and he always wanted Adrian and me to share his love of it, but I have to say, neither of us did. Well, Adrian was just a little boy then, so he didn't really dislike it, but it terrified me to have him out there with guns and the like." Her eyes were bugged out, and her cheeks were red.

"Good news then, I assume your husband took his hunting gear with him, so there are no hunting rifles in the house. Which means you can't have been the person who shot at me."

Bitsy went back to wringing her hands and glanced

nervously at her son. "There aren't exactly no hunting rifles in the house. Um ... well..."

"Dear old Dad peeled out of Maple Hills so fast, he left skid marks on the road. All kinds of his stuff is in the house, and he never came back for it. Never came back for anything or anyone," Adrian said, concern in his eyes as he looked over at his mother.

"I'm sorry," I murmured.

He waved his hands. "It's okay. He doesn't deserve us anyway."

Bitsy straightened her spine. "That's just not true, sweetie pie. Your father is a good man—"

She obviously was winding up to extol all of her ex-husband's virtues, but Adrian cut her off with a sharp glance and a snort of derision.

"He doesn't deserve the dirt on the bottom of your shoes, Mom. You're worth a million of him."

Her eyes glistened with tears, and she clasped her hands together. "Oh, Adrian, you're such a good boy."

"Yeah, yeah." Adrian shifted awkwardly in his chair to look at Jeremy and me. "But here's the thing, since he took off without a backward glance, we've still got all of his old junk down in the basement. Including his hunting rifles."

Looked like we couldn't rule Bitsy out just yet.

Chapter Eighteen

"Be a good girl." I settled Fluffy's travel carrier between a portable heater and the crates of apples and jugs of cider behind the Maple Hills Orchard table at the Fall Festival.

"Is she ever?" Dylan's brother Danny, aka Chief Carlow, asked with a devilish grin.

"She is always a good girl," I said staunchly, and was rewarded from snickers from Danny's two teenaged daughters and even Dylan. I put my hands on my hips and pivoted to face my boyfriend. "Et tu, Brutus?"

"Sorry, you know I love Fluffy, but it was funny." He shrugged and handed a bag of shiny, red apples across the table to a customer, who was quickly replaced by the next person in line.

"It's busy tonight," I observed.

"Saturday night is always the busiest night of the festival, because of the fireworks later," Dylan said.

I caught a movement off to my right and pasted a cheery smile on my face, "May I help you?" The smile faded.

"Hello, Amanda." Mallory stood on the other side of the table with Nesbitt Sharpley-Smythe. The couple were dressed like they were in an expensive store's 'Autumn in New England' catalog. Plaid, tweed, and in Mallory's case, buttery soft leather boots that came up above the knee of her skinny jeans.

"I didn't expect to see you both here tonight. It doesn't seem like your idea of a hot Saturday night."

"When in Rome." Nesbitt shrugged.

"And, really, what else is there to do in Maple Hills?" Mallory sneered.

"Did you want to buy something, or are you just here to be snarky about our hometown?"

"I'd like one of the hot mulled ciders. Would you like one too, my dear?" Nesbitt touched Mallory's hand with a brief, featherlight movement, which I guess passed as PDA in some circles.

"Yes, please."

"Two mulled ciders coming up," I said.

As I turned around to pour two cups of cider from the urn which was keeping the cinnamon-scented beverage warm, Nesbitt cleared his throat. I glanced over my shoulder at him.

"Dylan, if you can spare a moment, I'd like to speak to you," he said.

"If you're here to make another offer on my land, it's not the time." Dylan shook his head as he handed a box of maple sugar candy to a little girl.

I grimaced as I realized we'd both been so busy, I hadn't had the opportunity to tell Dylan about Nesbitt's visit.

"The polar opposite, actually." A small smile tilted up Nesbitt's mouth, but didn't reach his cold eyes.

Dylan regarded the man for a long moment and then

bobbed his head. "I can take a few minutes." He turned to his brother. "Danny, can you and the girls hold down the fort while Amanda and I talk to these two?"

"Of course, what do you think, you're indispensable? Go." Danny flapped his hands.

"Um, I wasn't invited. I can stay and help man the table," I said.

"No, I want you with me." Dylan put his hand on the small of my back and guided me out from behind the table.

When we passed Fluffy's crate, she yipped in a frantic manner. I paused and murmured to her, "Don't worry, Fluff. I'm not leaving you. I'm just stepping away for a couple of minutes."

One corner of Mallory's ruby lips tilted up, and she arched her perfect eyebrows.

"What? She has abandonment issues," I said as I brushed past her.

The four of us walked until we were far enough away from the noisy festival that we could talk and be heard comfortably.

Nesbitt sipped his cider. "Delicious."

"Thank you, but as you can see, it's very busy here and I don't want to leave my brother and nieces alone for too long. What did you want to discuss?" Dylan's voice was polite, but firm.

"No pleasantries then? Fine. I wanted to let you know on Monday you will be receiving documents rescinding my offer for your land."

Dylan drew in a sharp breath. "A formal document isn't necessary. We never came to an agreement. You made your offers repeatedly, and I turned you down every time."

Nesbitt inclined his head as he took another sip of aromatic cider. "Fair point, but I like to dot every 'i' and cross every 't'. It's never a good idea to leave an opening for a lawsuit."

I suppressed a laugh and slanted a glance at Dylan, who looked bemused. "Dylan? Sue to force you to honor your unwanted offer for his land? I don't think so."

Mallory smirked at Nesbitt. "For once, I've got to agree with Amanda. It's not how Dylan rolls."

"Out of curiosity, are you making an offer to someone else in town?" Dylan asked, ignoring us both.

"No one else in town owns enough land to accommodate our development. Mallory is already researching other areas, and has found a place in ... where was it again?" Nesbitt waved his hand gracefully, and looked to Mallory to supply the name.

"New Hampshire," she replied.

He snapped his fingers. "Right, New Hampshire. There's a retiring farmer ready to sell his land. A wise man. He'll be able to live like a king in a warmer climate for the rest of his life. I would've preferred Maple Hills, but you've made it clear you're not interested and never will be."

An awkward silence ensued, which Dylan broke when he jerked his head at the orchard's table. "Thank you for letting me know, but Amanda and I need to get back to work now."

"Certainly. Enjoy your evening." Nesbitt nodded amiably and strolled toward the festival.

"It was nice seeing you again, Dylan. Maybe we can get together before I leave town?" Mallory ran her hand up his arm.

Seriously? Right in front of me? The woman was shameless. And this time she couldn't even pretend she was coming on to Dylan for his land, but she was barking up the wrong tree.

"I don't think so, Mallory. Best of luck in New Hampshire, and good bye." Dylan nodded curtly and took my hand.

She turned on her heel and followed Nesbitt without even a glance in my direction.

Dylan took a step, but I stayed rooted in place.

"What's up, Amanda?"

I took a deep breath, my brow furrowed. "They seem anxious to get out of town."

"The Connecticut State Police might have something to say about them leaving," Dylan said.

"True, but it makes me wonder. They were so set on your land for this development, and all of sudden, they've changed their mind and Mallory has found a location in another state? It's suspicious. Like they're trying to break all ties to Maple Hills and get out fast. The way a murderer might want to do."

ONCE THE SUN SET, THE AIR CHILLED EVEN MORE, AND I was grateful for the portable heaters Dylan had brought for our booth. Fluffy was settled next to one, and wore an autumnal orange sweater. She looked cozy and content when I peeked in her carrier.

"How is The Beast doing?"

I jumped at the unexpected sound of Aunt Lori's voice behind me. I stood and held my hands over my heart. "Jeez, scare me to death, why doncha? Fluffy is doing fine."

Hitch stood next to my aunt with his arm draped around her shoulders. "Can we get two of the hot mulled ciders, please?"

"Coming right up," I said as I grabbed two cups and filled them. "Having fun at the festival?"

"We are. I always enjoy the Fall Festival." Aunt Lori reached out and took the cup I held out to her, while Hitch took his.

"I'm looking forward to a hot drink. It's really cold tonight." Hitch shivered.

"You're only cold because you never emerge from your warm, cozy bar long enough to experience the outside temps. The weather isn't too bad." Lori bumped her hip against his.

"The only bummer so far tonight is Detective Panchak is here. He was giving me the hairy eyeball earlier." Hitch screwed up his mouth.

"Are you any closer to catching the killer?" Lori asked me.

I shrugged. "I feel like I have all the pieces of the puzzle, but I just can't fit them together yet. Hopefully, it will all click into place soon."

"I thought I saw Adrian Van Dyke earlier, so Bitsy must be around here somewhere. I wonder if Detective Panchak is scowling at her too?" Lori said.

I furrowed my brow. "I'm surprised Adrian is here, because Bitsy left town this afternoon for a conference she's attending."

"Are you sure? Because I'm pretty sure it was Adrian we saw. It was a young man, holding a cane, and he's the only one I know in town who does," Hitch said.

"Jeremy and I stopped by their house earlier today, and … " I leaned across the table and lowered my voice. "She also told us they still have her ex-husband's hunting rifles in their house."

Lori's green eyes widened. "Highly suspicious."

Hitch bobbed his head side to side. "Not necessarily.

Lots of folks in town have hunting rifles. It doesn't mean she was the one taking potshots at Amanda. Seriously, can you picture mousey, little Bitsy hiding in the woods at night and shooting at Amanda and The Beast?"

"Fluffy," I corrected automatically. "It does seem far-fetched, but she might just be at the end of her rope and snapped."

A man stepped up behind Lori. She glanced over her shoulder and then leaned across the table to kiss my cheek. Her lips were warm on my icy skin. "Looks like we're holding up the line. See you later. Maybe for the fireworks?"

"We'll look for you guys," I said and waved as they strolled away, sipping their mulled ciders.

"I'll take one of those hot ciders, please. It's colder than a witches'... er ... well ... you know what, tonight," The man said in a booming voice.

I recognized the Chicago accent before I even looked at his face. Gary Bullaro. "Hello, Mr. Bullaro. One mulled cider, coming up."

"Oh, it's you, I keep seeing you all over the place."

I smiled at him as I handed over his drink. "It's a small town. You can't avoid people even if you want to. That will be five dollars please."

He put his cider down on the table and pulled his wallet out of his back pocket, and passed me a five. "A person can get lost in the city, and I like the privacy. One thing my stay here has taught me is I am not made for the country. Give me the city every time. I can't wait to get home."

"Hopefully, you'll be able to leave soon, but I'm sorry you're not enjoying your stay in Maple Hills. Maybe under better circumstances, you'd like it more."

"Maybe, maybe not." He winked at me. "You have a good night."

I stared at him as he meandered over to a booth with pumpkins and Halloween decorations for sale. Gary Bullaro had fallen off the top of my suspect list, but his comments made me wonder if I'd eliminated him too soon.

It was odd the number one thing he missed about the city was the anonymity. It would be easy to murder someone in a big city and then blend into the scenery, whereas in tiny Maple Hills, he stood out like the last green leaf on a maple tree.

"Amanda, you have a customer waiting," Danny called from the other end of the table, where he grabbed a bag of apples.

I pushed my inner sleuth to the side and let the apple seller come to the forefront again. With a bright smile at the family on the other side of the table, I asked, "What can I get for you folks?"

"Maple sugar candy!" A little girl squealed.

THE CROWD THINNED AS IT GOT TO BE CLOSER TO TIME FOR the fireworks display. I glanced at Dylan. "Would it be all right if I took a break and ran Fluffy home now? Fireworks are not her friend."

"Of course. We're just closing up now. I'll wait for you here, and we can head over to watch the fireworks when you get back." He bent down to give me a quick kiss, and I leaned into his warmth and shivered.

"I am definitely using the heated seats in the car on the way home. They didn't get a lot of use when I lived in southern California, but they're getting a workout this fall."

He chuckled and went back to work. I leaned down to talk to Fluffy. "Do you want a quick bathroom break before we head home?"

She stood up and shook and gazed at me with an avid expression. "I'll take those big eyes as a 'yes'. There's a spot designated for dogs over that way. C'mon, girl. We'll hit it, and then get you safely home before the big booms start." I opened the portable crate and clipped her leash on her. "I'll be back in a few for her crate," I called out to Dylan.

Fluffy pranced ahead of me; her plumed tail held high over her back.

The dog rest area was set apart from the rest of the festival, and was dimly lit. I remembered the last time we were in a dark, wooded area at night so Fluffy could do her business and shuddered. Since the shooting, we'd stuck pretty close to the house for her bathroom breaks. Like a quick sprint to the door close, in case bullets started flying again.

Fluffy seemed to feel no such apprehension, as she paused and sniffed every tree and stone. I gazed up at the stars, twinkling in the clear night sky.

My thoughts drifted back to the case. If I opened my mind and reviewed what I knew, maybe the missing piece of the puzzle would fall into place. My molars ground together, and I shook my head. Nope. Concentrating too hard wasn't helping.

Instead, maybe I should try to just let my mind float free, not grasping onto every fact and suspicion. I inhaled fully, and exhaled slowly to calm my mind.

After a few moments, my eyes popped open wide and I straightened up, because it had actually worked. The last piece clicked into place so firmly, I was surprised I couldn't hear an audible kerchunk sound.

I knew who the killer was.

From the trees ahead of me came a rustling sound, and my heart caught in my chest. I flashed back to the night we'd been shot at, but maybe I was overreacting. Fluffy raised her head, peered in the same direction, and growled. I inhaled sharply. It definitely wasn't my imagination.

"Is someone there?" My voice was firm and confident, in spite of the fact my legs shook like jelly.

More rustling was the only response, and Fluffy erupted in frantic barking.

I squinted as I looked into the dark copse of trees and caught a flash of movement. "I see you there. Who is it?"

"It's your worst nightmare."

I gulped as my suspicions were confirmed, and I recognized the voice of the person who murdered Dennis Millikan.

Chapter Nineteen

The deep chuckle that followed those ominous words filled my heart with dread. This was a person who'd killed once, and had shot at Fluffy and me.

Fluffy dug in her heels and tugged hard to advance toward the threat to protect us. My girl was so brave, but she was no match for a gun. I gripped the canvas leash, and knew I'd have rope burns on my palm in the morning.

"You can come out in the open, Adrian. I know it's you." I willed my voice to remain steady.

The rustling grew louder, until Adrian Van Dyke emerged from the trees, a rifle pointed directly at me.

The blood raced from my head to my feet so fast, I was afraid I'd pass out, but doing so would be a death sentence for Fluffy and me. I had to stay conscious and sharp to keep us both alive. I breathed deeply to calm my racing pulse.

"You're a very smart woman. I knew you were close to figuring it all out." His smile chilled me to the core.

I moved to squat down and pick up Fluffy, but he snapped out a command. "Don't move."

"Can I pick up my dog?"

"No."

I needed to keep him talking to buy time. Hopefully, someone else would need to walk a dog soon, and come to this isolated section of the town green. "I haven't figured it all out, maybe you could fill in the pieces for me?"

"Why?" He snorted. "I'm just going to kill you."

"Then I'd know what happened before I die. Please?"

As I'd hoped, his ego couldn't resist the chance to show off, and Adrian stood a little taller. "I was very clever."

Before I could respond, Aunt Lori's voice called out loud and clear and all-too-close to the unstable man with the gun.

"Dylan sent me to look for you, Amanda. He said you were gone a long time. And you were right, I saw Adrian—" her voice trailed off at the end of the sentence as she reached us. Her eyes were huge on her pale face. She began to pivot on her heels, but Adrian swung the gun toward her.

"You're not going anywhere, Ms. Seldon. Not now. I'm sorry, because you've always been nice to me at the library. But you're going to have to die now too. Get over next to your niece." He waved the gun in my direction.

Lori edged closer and grasped my hand when she reached my side. I gave it a reassuring squeeze I was far from feeling, but I needed to keep her calm. If either of us lost our marbles, it could trigger Adrian into acting rashly and shooting indiscriminately.

"Adrian was just about to tell me how he killed Dennis Millikan."

She gasped and looked at the young man with the weapon trained on us.

He giggled, a high-pitched sound, and I wondered if he wasn't quite sane. Had he always been off, or had the accident caused it? I hoped I lived long enough to find out which.

"No, no, no." He smirked and waved the gun playfully. "The man with the rifle makes the rules." He jerked the rifle in my direction. "You first. How did you figure it out?"

"I hadn't even considered you until recently. I suspected your mother more than you."

"My mother? A killer? Only of my spirit." He snorted and said, "Carry on with your story."

I cleared my throat. Fluffy cast a quick glance over her shoulder at me, but turned right back to growl at Adrian. She looked less than fierce in her doggie sweater, but her face showed she was ready to take on any enemy. "A couple of things occurred to me tonight. When I heard you were at the festival, I couldn't' imagine how you got here, since your mother is out of town and couldn't drive you. But then I remembered Jeremy told me you didn't drive because you lost your license, and not because you weren't physically able to. It didn't register with me at the time, because I didn't suspect you. But I realized tonight if you can drive, it's possible you were the person who drove your mother's car to Millikan's the night he was killed."

"You're right. It was me." He raised his eyebrows in surprise.

"No need to look so surprised, my niece is very smart," Aunt Lori said. "I can't believe Bitsy would let you take her car when you don't have a license. How did you manage it?"

He giggled again, and I shivered. "I put one of my pain prescriptions in her evening cup of herbal tea. She was yawning up a storm, went to bed early, and was out for the night. So, I was able to slip out and take her car without her ever knowing."

"You gave her a pill strong enough to knock her out for the night? She could've died!" I exclaimed.

"It was a risk I was willing to take." Adrian shrugged, and scrunched up his face. "There must've been more than the car. What else made you suspect me?"

"It was when we were at your house. You told Jeremy and me about your college friends; how you met because you were all in the science department. Which meant you might know about poisons. I planned to question you more about what you studied tomorrow, to see if I was right."

"You were. I'm a chemistry major. I knew as little as half a teaspoon of an aconite root tincture hidden in alcohol would kill a man. And it's hard to detect. In a little hick town like this one, I didn't think the police would be able to conduct the sort of toxicology analysis necessary. One of my fraternity brothers swiped some from the chem lab and brought it to me. No questions asked. Man, I miss those guys." His voice trailed off sadly, and after a brisk shake of his head, he continued. "I didn't count on Chief Carlow having to hand the case over to the state police, which happened because your boyfriend is a suspect, right?"

I nodded once. "Yep. Clearing Dylan's name was the reason I started investigating, so I guess you could say it was the fatal flaw in your plan."

"Very true." He pouted. "It was a very clever plan. I thought it was flawless."

"One thing I don't understand is why Millikan let you into the house, and how you were able to slip the tincture in his drink?"

Aunt Lori squeezed my hand. We hadn't let go of each

other yet. It was like a lifeline. "I was wondering what excuse you used to get inside too. It's not like you were friends or something. And your mother despised him."

"She's fixated on my situation. It's oppressive, and I couldn't stand it anymore. Since Dad took off, she was always a little overly-attentive, but after the accident? She smothered me. Wouldn't let me do the smallest things. It's like she enjoyed treating me like a baby. But I hated it!"

"It would be difficult," I murmured.

"Difficult doesn't begin to describe it. She blamed my fraternity brothers for my partying, and I think she was determined to not let me go back to school until my buddies graduated. And then she fixated on Dennis. But after a while, I started to see her point about him. I was clearly bombed the night I wrecked the car, but he kept pouring and pouring. Even gave me tequila shots on the house, because he said I was such a good customer. While I recuperated, I had nothing to do but think, and I realized Mom was right. All my problems were Millikan's fault. And I started to plan."

"So what happened the night he died? You never answered Aunt Lori's question."

He sniffed. "Right. So, he'd always liked me. The town didn't open up to him and Oh Denny Boy's. Everyone insisted on going to Hitchcock's Tavern. And then the new hotel opened their fancy cocktail bar, and it took away what little business he had. I only went to Oh Denny Boy's when I was home on break because I was less likely to run into my mother or her friends there."

"So he let you into his condo because he thought you were his friend?" I asked.

"Pfft. Idiot. Yep. He did just what I expected, asked me inside and offered me something to drink. He said he had just bought some of those new hard ciders from the orchard and offered me one. I told him I couldn't drink alcohol with my meds, but for him to go ahead. Which wasn't exactly true. I just didn't want anyone to realize there was an unaccounted for bottle of cider. Pretty clever, huh?"

"Very smart," I forced myself to say, when I was really thinking *very devious*.

"Thanks. He gave me an apple instead, which I didn't eat. He laughed and said an apple would be good for me, because an apple a day keeps the doctor away. It infuriated me. I could eat a dozen apples a day and I'd still be forced to see all my doctors every week, and it was all his fault. So he opened his drink, and I made some small talk. Then I snuffled a bunch, pretended to sneeze, and asked him for a tissue. He said they were in the bathroom, but I waved my cane, looked pathetic, and said it wasn't easy for me to get around." Adrian emitted another high-pitched laugh. "As I assumed, his guilt took over and he was all, 'I'll get it for you, don't get up'. Sucker. Once he was out of the room, I used an eye dropper to put the tincture in his open cider. I can move pretty good when I need to, which is why it's so ridiculous my mother insists on keeping me home for another semester."

"And he didn't taste it?" Lori asked.

"Nope. After he gave me the tissue, he slugged back a good bit of his drink. I knew I needed to get out of there, before he died, so I said I had to get home before my mom realized I wasn't there. That I'd just wanted to stop by to let him know there were no hard feelings on my part."

"How did he end up in the backyard?" I wrinkled my nose. It was one thing which had puzzled me from the start.

"I knew nosey old Mrs. Prattleworth lived across the way, and didn't want her to see me. I figured if she recognized the car, she'd assume it was Mom, but if she saw me then my whole plan was shot. I admired the view and asked to leave out the back door so I could see the lake. I didn't expect him to come too. He seemed worried about me walking down the stairs and on the grass. Dennis grabbed the apple off the table and said he'd eat if I didn't want it, and we left out the back."

"Did he walk you to the car?" I asked.

"No, I didn't want him to. He was so loud, I was afraid neighbors would hear him, look to see what it was, and see me. I convinced him I was fine, and left him out back."

"With his cider and the apple, which I found by his body."

"Yep."

There was an awkward pause, as my brain whirred trying to think of a way out of our current predicament. There were two of us, plus my attack shih tzu, and only one of him. Could we overpower him before he had time to shoot one of us?

Adrian heaved a sigh. "You know, you both are real nice ladies, and I don't want to do it, but I have to kill you. The dog first though, because it would start yapping and draw attention and I wouldn't get out of here in time."

"The gunshots will draw attention to us too," I pointed out.

"I could wait for the fireworks to start, I guess."

"Then you wouldn't have to kill Fluffy. No one will hear her over them either," I said.

"You're trying to talk me out of killing her. You really love the little rat, don't you?" he asked.

"I do."

"I wanted to get a dog, but Mom didn't like the idea. She said it would be too much work for her."

Another silence ensued, as I pondered how long we

had until the fireworks started and Adrian started shooting. We had to make a move before then, because much as I wanted Fluffy to live if Lori and I couldn't, my Plan A was for *all* of us to get out of here alive.

I caught a glimpse of movement in the trees behind Adrian. I struggled to keep my expression neutral, because I realized the cavalry had arrived in the form of Detective Panchak, and I'd never been so happy to see the man in my life.

LORI'S HAND GRIPPED MINE IN A SUDDEN MOVE, AND I KNEW she saw him too. I tried to mentally will her to be silent.

Panchak must've realized we'd spotted him, because he held his left index finger over his lips. I glimpsed a gun in his right hand. Lori's hand relaxed, and I could tell she was playing it cool too.

Unfortunately, Fluffy didn't get the memo, and when she spotted the detective, she lurched forward toward him, barking like a wolf on the hunt, but looking like a pampered lapdog in her pumpkin sweater.

"What's your rat doing? What's happening?" Adrian whipped his head around, and I let go of Fluffy's leash.

My girl didn't fail me. My brain knew she was just trying to get to Panchak, but my heart liked to think what she did next was calculated to save us. Hey, a dog owner can dream, right? Because Fluffy did the best possible thing. She knocked Adrian's cane out of his hand on her way past him, and it dropped to the ground. He wobbled, and Lori and I ran forward as if we'd rehearsed the maneuver. She grabbed the arm which had held his cane, and I picked up the cane and whopped his gun arm with it as hard as I could. It worked, and when he dropped the gun, I grabbed his arm and twisted it behind his back.

Panchak's footsteps thundered as he raced from the tree line. "Freeze, Van Dyke. Hands in the air."

Since Lori and I had his arms pinned, Adrian was not able to comply.

"Stand down, ladies. I've got it from here," Panchak said as he dodged by Fluffy's flashing teeth to grab Adrian.

As the adrenaline slowed, my legs buckled just the teensiest bit. When I watched Panchak cuff Adrian and read him his rights, I developed a new appreciation for the good detective.

Chapter Twenty

Dylan, Danny, and Hitch ran towards us, with Jeremy, Eric, Cara, and Mitch hot on their heels. My parents brought up the rear.

I ran to Dylan and he caught me in a tight embrace. It was almost enough to squeeze the breath out of me, but I didn't mind. Now the danger was over, shock had set in, and my body trembled.

Fluffy barked in the background and pulled me out of the moment. "Oh no! The fireworks are going to start soon. Detective Panchak, may I bring Fluffy home before they start?"

As the dog in question currently danced around Adrian and Panchak, nipping at their feet, he said, "Please get her out of here. Just come down to the station right after. I need to get your statement."

I saluted him. "I promise."

As I ran to retrieve Fluffy, all my family and friends were talking at once, trying to figure out what the heck was happening.

"I'll drive you," Dylan said.

"Thanks." I squatted on the ground next to Fluffy, and glanced over my shoulder to flash him a smile.

"Chief Carlow, could you secure the crime scene, while I take him to the station?" Panchak asked.

"Of course," Danny said, and immediately began to herd everyone away from the scene.

As Hitch led Lori toward the municipal parking lot, she blew a kiss in my direction. "Good work, Mandy-bel. I'll see you at the station."

~

"DOES ANYONE WANT ANOTHER PANCAKE?" MY DAD ASKED from the griddle in our kitchen.

It was late by the time Aunt Lori and I had given our statements, and we were starving. My mom came to the rescue and had texted to say everyone was waiting at home for us, and my folks were making pancakes. Apple pancakes, of course. It was October in New England after all, and her daughter was dating the owner of an orchard.

"I do," Jeremy jumped up with his empty plate.

I snickered, and he shrugged. "What? I'm a stress eater, you know that about me."

Cara and Mitch had to go home with their kids, but I promised Cara I would stop by her house and fill her in first thing tomorrow. The Rosenbergs, Hitch, Aunt Lori, Jeremy, and Eric rounded up the group around the kitchen table, while my mom fried bacon and my dad flipped pancakes. The delectable aromas of coffee, bacon, and cinnamon apples filled the air, and it was so blissful, there was a distinct possibility Adrian had actually killed me on the town green and I was in heaven now.

"I can't believe Adrian Van Dyke is a murderer. Bitsy is

going to be devastated." Mrs. Rosenberg shook her head mournfully.

"Not to mention he drugged her to get out of the house to kill Millikan." Aunt Lori waved a piece of turkey bacon in the air as she spoke. Since my dad's surgery, pork products were verboten in my parent's house.

"And Adrian had the nerve to use his one phone call to ask her to get him a lawyer, and she did," Danny said.

"What we won't do for our kids, am I right?" Mr. Rosenberg asked.

"Panchak told me her flight had just landed in Columbus for the conference, and she was trying to get on the first available flight back, so I guess you're right," Aunt Lori said.

"I wonder what she'll do. Do you think she'll stay in town?" I asked.

"Where would she go?" My mom shrugged. "And she did nothing wrong."

"Aside from smothering her only child until he cracked and turned into a cold-blooded killer," Jeremy said.

"Speaking of the cold-blooded killer, good job finding another murderer and taking him down. Are you angling for my job?" Danny winked at me.

I held up both hands. "Definitely not. I just didn't want Dylan or Hitch to go to jail for a crime they didn't commit."

"And I for one am most grateful." Hitch hoisted his coffee cup in a toast.

"Me too." Dylan's arm was draped across the back of my chair, and he squeezed my shoulder.

"You are both very welcome, but Fluffy and I are officially hanging up our sleuthing hats. I'm looking forward to a nice, peaceful holiday season here in Maple Hills. I picked up a brochure for Santa's Christmas Village the other day. I can't wait!"

"And since the autumn rush will be over at the orchard, I'll really be able to enjoy it with you. Maybe we can do one of those horse-drawn sleigh rides together," Dylan said.

My cheeks heated up. As a teenager, I'd dreamed about going on a sleigh ride with Dylan but didn't think he even knew who I was. Looked like sixteen-year old Amanda's dreams were about to come true. "I would love it. And hopefully, Fluffy and I will be settled in our condo by then. I can't wait to decorate it for Christmas."

Fluffy snuffled at my feet, and I snuck her a tiny piece of pancake. My mother put her hands on her hips and scowled at me. "Amanda, you know she's not supposed to have people food."

"I know, but she deserves a little reward for tonight." I glanced down at Fluffy, who had gobbled down the pancake and looked up expectantly for me. "You were a very good girl tonight, knocking down the bad man's cane."

"Even I have to admit The Beast did good tonight. She gave us the opening we needed," Aunt Lori said.

"I for one would be very grateful for a quiet holiday season. Having your daughter face off against two killers in four months has been more action than I want to have," Dad said as he flipped two pancakes on his own plate and squeezed in next to me to finally eat his own meal.

"I'm done sleuthing. I mean it's Maple Hills, what are the odds there will be a third murder this year?" I asked.

Of course, I realize now I'd just been tempting fate, and should've stuffed another apple pancake in my mouth to keep myself from talking. Because the holiday season turned out to be anything but peaceful, and Fluffy and I were once again in the thick of it.

≈

DID YOU ENJOY AMANDA AND FLUFFY'S SLEUTHING adventures? If so, please take a minute to leave a rating or review on your favorite book site. Thank you!

≈

AND IF YOU MISSED *THE SLAY'S THE THING* DOWNLOAD IT today to see where it all began!

≈

IN THE MEANTIME, TRY A VISIT TO PORT SUNSET, FLORIDA. A Gulf Coast town inhabited by fun-loving, quirky residents, but with an unfortunate body count. Take a peek at book one in my Port Sunset Cozy Mystery series, *Penthouse, Pools, and Poison* ...

"ANOTHER CRISIS AVERTED. THANKS TO YOU, ELLIS." I slurped the last of my iced hazelnut coffee through the straw in the to-go cup and leaned against the padded wall of the hotel's service elevator.

The weathered face of the Gulf Palms Resort and Spa's maintenance man creased as he grinned at me. Ellis Smith was a notorious curmudgeon, and his smiles were as rare as snow in Port Sunset, Florida. But, for some reason, he'd always had a soft spot for me, and I'm super fond of the older man too—like an honorary uncle. The crazy uncle no one ever talks about in company, but my favorite, nonetheless.

"No problem, Millie. I'm just glad they noticed the leaky pipe in the backroom of the gift shop before it caused any real damage." His deep voice rumbled, and I heard the hint of a northern accent, in spite of all the decades he'd lived here in Port Sunset, Florida. A refugee from Connecticut winters myself, I recognized the slight accent as possibly being from northern New England.

His background was a mystery. Ellis did not like to talk about the past. He didn't like to talk much, period. He liked me better than anyone else at the hotel, and even I couldn't get him to open up to me.

The elevator binged right before the doors slid open. Ellis held the door back from automatically closing with one hand, and gestured for me to get out before him with the other. I flashed him a grin as I scooted out of the elevator into the grand, marble lobby of the Gulf Palms. Stan the bellman waited outside the service elevator, with a rolling luggage cart filled to overflowing, and Ellis held up his hand like a traffic cop and growled at Stan to keep him from pushing ahead of me to board the elevator. Seriously. Ellis growled. Like I said, he liked me better than anyone else at the hotel.

Stan fought against a grin and lost. As I stepped up next to him, he said out of the corner of his mouth, "What's your secret with Ellis? You're the only one he treats like a human being."

I shrugged. "Must be my natural charm."

To be honest, I think it was because I talked to Ellis when I first started working here. I didn't know he had a reputation for keeping to himself. Okay, keeping to himself is an understatement. He had a reputation for being a complete and total crabby hermit. I just talked to him like I would anyone else, and he didn't rebuff me the way he did other people, and over time we became good friends.

Stan laughed, but lingered in the lobby, as the elevator doors closed.

The gleaming marble lobby was blindingly white, and the windows looking over the Gulf of Mexico let in all the bright Florida sunshine. The lobby was decorated in the hotel's trademark pink and green, just like my work uniform capri pants, which were pink with little green palm trees embroidered on them. The Gulf Palms Resort managed to walk the line between comfortably welcoming and grand. Usually music played quietly in the lobby, either piped in over the sound system, or performed by a pianist at the grand piano tucked away in a corner by the Swaying Palms Bar. However, right now, the sounds reaching my ears were a lot less melodic.

"I thought the Gulf Palms Resort was supposed to be a class place, not some rinky-dink operation!" The man's face was red as a beet, as he yelled at the young woman behind the check-in desk.

"Who's the heart attack waiting to happen?" I whispered out of the corner of my mouth to Stan, as he leaned around me and pressed the call button for the elevator again.

"Eugene Tarkington. His family checked in last night after you left. I was just watching the show, but I better get these bags up to their owners." He winked at me as he rolled the cart onto the service elevator. "Let me know how it turns out."

I took one last bracing sip of my iced coffee, and tossed the empty to-go cup into the trash next to the elevator, as the doors slid shut on Stan. I frowned at the scene before me. The woman working the desk this morning was little more than a kid, a college student, who worked here part-time. What kind of bully would be talking to her this way?

"I better go help Emily," I said in a low voice to Ellis, who stared at the sight in the lobby through eyes fit to bug out of his head.

He cleared his throat, and his voice was gravely and low when he replied, "Good luck. You're gonna need it."

"Thanks." I crinkled my nose as I peered at Ellis. He normally ignored the guests as much as possible, and as a result, was never rattled by this type of outburst. I wondered what was up with him, but couldn't take the time to get to the bottom of the mystery right now. Usually, I loved my work in this beautiful tropical resort, but in this moment I wished I was anywhere else. I forced a smile as bright and cheerful as the lobby to my face as I approached the angry man. I knew the moment Emily spotted me, because her face brightened, in spite of the tears glistening in her eyes.

"May I be of assistance?" I asked in what I hoped was a cheerful tone, but the truth was I was angry enough to pop this guy in the nose for making Emily cry.

"Who the hell are you?" The man hollered. He was a big man, but soft looking. I knew the type all-too-well from working here. Rich, used to getting everything he wants, and unwelcome as a gator on a golf course.

"My name is Millie Wentworth, and I'm the Assistant General Manager of the Gulf Palms. What seems to be the problem, sir?"

"I don't deal with assistants. Where's the general manager?" The man demanded, looking over my head as he asked, as if expecting the general manager to appear out of thin air at his command.

"Mr. Clark is off the premises at the moment, but why

don't you let me know what's happening, and perhaps I can help you."

Little did the big loudmouth know, even if the GM, Vincent Clark, was here, he'd be hiding in his office right now, after delegating me to deal with the angry guest. Confrontation was not Vince's jam. My nickname around the resort was 'the Fixer', and I took pride in the fact there wasn't a discontented guest I couldn't soothe. At least up until now there wasn't.

The man huffed. "Fine. I'm Eugene Tarkington."

He paused at this point, as if he expected me to genuflect at the sound of his name.

"Nice to meet you, Mr. Tarkington," I replied, my professional smile still firmly in place, in spite of the fact I was sticking imaginary pins into my imaginary voodoo doll of Eugene.

The crimson red in his cheeks, had died down to a more subdued shade, but he was still clearly cheesed off. He jerked his thumb at a very attractive, younger woman behind him. Maybe his daughter?

"My wife—"

Nope. Not his daughter. A trophy wife. She was lovely, tall and statuesque, with perfectly coiffed and highlighted hair. She looked slightly bored with the scene before her, and she barely acknowledged my presence with a faint nod of her head, before she went back to inspecting her long fingernails.

"—wanted a manicure and pedicure at the spa this afternoon, and when she called down, she was told there were no appointments available until tomorrow." His voice rose, until the end of the sentence was back to the ear-splitting volume it had been when I'd arrived on the scene.

"I'm very sorry, Mr. Tarkington—"

"Sorry?!" He interrupted me with a bellow, and his

face was back to mid-summer, beefsteak tomato red again. He pointed at Emily behind the desk. "This one was sorry too. What good does sorry do? Sorry won't get my wife's nails done."

My smile faltered a bit, but I tried to keep my tone of voice upbeat and cheerful. "Let me call the Tranquility Spa, and see what I can do. Would you care for a glass of champagne while I do so?"

Before her husband could start yelling again, Mrs. Tarkington perked up at the magic word 'champagne', and said, "I would."

"Not for me, I'm more of a Scotch man," Mr. Tarkington said.

I smiled at the young woman behind the desk, "Emily, please get Mrs. Tarkington a glass of champagne, and Mr. Tarkington our finest Scotch from the bar." I turned to look at the problem guest, who looked somewhat appeased at this point. "If you'd wait here, I'm just going to nip behind the desk to my office and call the spa manager to get things straightened out for you."

"That's more like it. Action. That's what I expect from subordinates when I have a problem. Oh! And one more thing—the toilet in the master bedroom is running, not up to my standards, missie."

Mrs. Tarkington appeared to roll her eyes, but it was done so quickly, I couldn't be sure.

"Luckily for you, I happen to be with the best maintenance man in the business, and he can take care of your plumbing issue in no time." I flashed a cocky grin and jerked my thumb over my shoulder at Ellis.

Mr. Tarkington craned his head to look behind me and scowled. "I don't see anybody."

I turned to look and Ellis had vanished. Huh. Maybe the yelling stressed him out more than I'd realized. I wondered if Ellis suffered from PTSD. I frowned, and pulled my smartphone out of the pocket of my capri pants. "He must have had another matter to attend to. I'll text him, and ask him to get to the penthouse ASAP."

Tarkington grunted in response. What lovely manners. The old saying that money can't buy class, sprung to my mind. I wonder why?

As I hurried to a door just past the check-in desk that led to the management offices, I tapped out a quick text with my thumbs, asking Ellis to fix the running toilet as soon as he could. I held up a key card on my key chain, and opened the door after it beeped. I entered the second office on the left, which was mine. My boss scored the coveted big office behind the first door and a small conference room was at the end of the hall. I tossed my purse onto the desk, and didn't bother to turn on the lights, or even to sit down, as I suspected Mr. Tarkington was not a patient man. I hit the speed dial button on my desktop phone to reach the spa.

"Hi, it's Millie. I need Maria, stat. We have a defcon level angry guest whose wife wants a mani/pedi."

After being on hold for a few seconds, I heard the Cuban accented voice of Maria Garcia, the spa manager. "Let me guess...the Tarkingtons?"

"You're psychic, Maria. They made poor Emily cry. I'm plying them with expensive booze right now, what can you do for me?"

"Give me five minutes to see what I can do, and then bring her over. I'll do her stinking nails myself if I have to."

"I owe you."

"Yes. Yes you do," Maria said, but I could hear the smile in her voice.

"See you in five," I said before I hung up the desk

phone.

"Mr. Tarkington, we'll have someone from maintenance up to fix the running toilet at the earliest possible opportunity," I said with an admittedly phony, cheery smile.

"I should hope so," he blustered in return. Although, the glass of fine scotch he held seemed to have ratcheted down his anger a bit.

I turned my head to speak to the sullen looking Mrs. Tarkington. "And, if you'll please come with me, Mrs. Tarkington, we can head over to the Tranquility Spa. The manager is arranging things for you as we speak."

Mrs. Tarkington inclined her head in a regal manner, but with the air of a woman who was used to people jumping through hoops to give her what she wanted. "Thank you, Millie."

Her husband squinted at me over his crystal rocks glass. "Millie is a funny name for a young woman. It makes you sound like an old broad."

"I go by Millie, but I was named after my paternal grandmother, Mildred Wentworth," I replied, although my smile faltered around the edges a bit by this point. I turned back to Mrs. Tarkington and said, "You may bring your champagne with you." I swept my hand out to the far end of the lobby, "The spa entrance is on the left up ahead. After you."

"I'm going back up to sit by the private pool on our rooftop deck," Mr. Tarkington hollered after us. "Don't know why all of the kids are at the public pool and beach with the hoi polloi."

His wife shrugged with complete and total disinterest

and walked ahead of me towards the spa. She called over her shoulder, "I'll be back later. I might try to get a massage too, while I'm at the spa."

I flashed Mr. Tarkington one final smile, and scrambled to catch up with Mrs. Tarkington. The woman had to be almost six feet tall, and all legs. Even though her movements were languid, she was covering some serious distance with each step. At five foot six, I consider myself average height, but she towered over me. I wondered if she'd been a model when she met her husband. She had the look of one. I tugged self-consciously at my ponytail. I'd been running late this morning, and just pulled my brown hair back to save time, rather than styling it. I hoped I didn't look too much of a mess, although compared to Mrs. Tarkington, there weren't many women who wouldn't look a little frumpy.

"I think Millie is a sweet name," she said.

"Thank you," My eyes widened in surprise, at her words. They were the most she'd said so far, and were almost...kind. Not at all what I expected to hear from her.

"My husband doesn't always realize how he sounds, and people might take offense where none was intended. Like the 'old broad' comment before."

"No worries. He's right, it is kind of an old-fashioned name. My other grandmother is called Lulu."

Mrs. Tarkington smiled, and her appearance was transformed. She was truly lovely. "I think I'd be glad I was named Millie, after my other grandmother, in that case."

I raised one shoulder in a shrug, and warmth spread in the general vicinity of my heart at the thought of my beloved grandmother. "Lulu suits her. She's a real pip."

We reached the salon, and I held the door open for Mrs. Tarkington. I followed her into the spa lobby, where we were greeted by the soothing scent of lavender, and mellow, instrumental spa music. The sort of plinky-plinky New Age music they always played in spas.

A young, dark-skinned woman was at the front desk. Her hair was in long braids, which were tied back in a ponytail, and she wore the spa version of the Gulf Palms staff uniform. A tunic style jacket, with leggings, both in the trademark pink, with tiny, green palm trees on them. A sage green, and subdued pale pink, were the predominate colors of the spa's décor, and a large potted palm was in the center of the lobby area. Products available for sale were discreetly displayed on shelves built into the walls.

"Hello, Millie," the young woman greeted me, with a Caribbean lilt to her voice.

"Hiya, Tanya. This is—"

"Mrs. Tarkington," Another woman spoke as she entered from a glass door behind the front desk, which led to the salon. The petite, middle-aged woman came out from behind the desk, with her hand extended in greeting. She had dark hair pulled back in a bun, and spoke with a slight Cuban accent, "I'm Maria Garcia, the manager of Tranquility Spa and Salon. Welcome."

"Hello," Mrs. Tarkington answered, and held out her hand to limply and very briefly shake Maria's.

"I'm very sorry for any confusion about your appointment today." Maria gestured to a door on the other side of the front desk, just past the comfy seats in the waiting area. "The dressing rooms are through there. Tanya, please take Mrs. Tarkington, and let her change into a robe for her treatments." While she spoke, she removed the empty champagne flute from Mrs. Tarkington's hand. "Let me take care of that for you, ma'am. We'll have another glass waiting for you at your manicure station."

"Thank you," Mrs. Tarkington said, as she followed Tanya to the door. At the last moment, she turned and spoke as if it were an afterthought, "And thank you for your help with our problems today, Millie."

"You are very welcome," I said to the woman's back as she walked through the door, which closed with a thunk behind her, while I was still speaking.

Maria rolled her eyes, and spoke in a soft voice, "She's charming."

"Compared to her husband, she is," I whispered back, with a dramatic eye roll.

"Lulu was in this morning for a mani/pedi. Evidently, she has a hot date tonight."

I heaved a sigh. "It's a sad state of affairs, when my seventy-something grandmother has a more active social life than I do."

"You need to get out of this place more often. You work too hard," Maria waved the empty champagne glass at me.

"You're a fine one to talk. When's the last time you had a day off, huh?"

"Point taken," Maria said, "Hey, Lulu and her crew are by the pool. Why don't you take a break and head out to see her?"

"Good idea. I think I will. I want to find out who this hot date is with tonight."

~

TO KEEP READING, DOWNLOAD **PENTHOUSE, POOLS, & POISON** today.

AND CHECK OUT THE REST OF THE PORT SUNSET SERIES too, ***Diamonds, Dunes, & Death***, ***Sunshine, Selfies, & Smugglers***, and ***Cabanas, Cupids, & Corpses***.

Acknowledgments

Publishing a novel is a terrifying thing. You live with these characters for months on end and grow to love them. So when you send them out into the world of readers it's scary. Which is why I want to thank my loyal readers for all your support over the years. You might not realize it, but some days your positive reviews, good ratings, and kind words on social media are what get me back to keyboard. So thank you from the bottom of my heart for going along on this ride with me for 11 books now. Cozy mystery readers rock!

And to the usual suspects—my beloved husband, Leo, my sisters, Judy and Mary, and my amazing writer friends, Claire Marti, Sharon Buchbinder, Peggy Jaeger, Judith Marshall. You've all been with me from the start of my writing career and are the best support group around. And this time, I literally would not have finished this book had it not been for Claire's 'gentle' encouragement. I appreciate your support and your hard truths when I needed to hear them too. You're the best!

About the Author

Louise Stevens is the author of the Port Sunset Mysteries, and the Second Act Cozy Mystery series. A lover of mysteries since her discovery of Nancy Drew many years ago, she is thrilled to be writing cozy mysteries now. She lives in Maryland with her husband, who also loves a good mystery, in a house packed with books.

Louise Stevens is the pen name of contemporary romance author Donna Simonetta.

Made in United States
Cleveland, OH
21 April 2025

16269257R00132